Withdrawn

RIVER MUSIC

river music

LEIGH SAUERWEIN

namelos

South Hampton, New Hampshire

Library of Congress Control Number: 2014941719

ISBN 978-1-60898-186-1 (hardcover: alk. paper)
ISBN 978-1-60898-187-8 (paperback: alk. paper)
ISBN 978-1-60898-188-5 (ebook)

www.namelos.com

In memory of my mother's voice

Contents

RIVER MUSIC

Rainy

When the girl from the valley came again, it was full summer. Rainy had felt kind of uneasy the night before, like something was about to happen, and she had found herself awake before sunup and had gone to stand at the front window of the house, looking out toward the pines. Sure enough, after a few minutes, there she came, just a shadow at first, moving up between the trees. But soon Rainy could see her clearly, thin and dark, in a pale blue dress, with that wild frizzy hair. At the edge of the woods the girl hesitated, then darted forward like a deer. Stopping in front of the house, she dug into the pocket of her dress and placed something on the bottom step. Then turned at once and ran, disappearing quickly into the pines.

Rainy felt her heart beating fast as she went to lift the latch and pull open the door. Papa Will and Ben wouldn't know; they were already out at work hoeing the cornfield. A knot formed in her stomach as she wondered what it would be this time.

The first time had been in the early spring. Rainy hadn't seen anybody at all. She had been poling the beans in their vegetable garden, and had suddenly discovered a shiny silver medallion and chain lying on the ground at the end of the row, as if it had been quickly flung there. A silver oval on a silver chain. Will and Ben had been way over on the other side of the wheat field, too far for a shout. It was like a tiny miracle had happened just to her. She had leaned down quickly and picked the necklace up, turning the oval medallion around and around in her dirt-stained fingers. It was the most delicate thing she had ever seen, engraved on both sides with a whirling pattern of lilies. And then she had pushed it hurriedly down into the pocket of her overalls and hadn't mentioned it to Will at all, or to Ben either, even though he was as close to her as any real brother. She had kept the necklace with her, hiding it under her mattress at night and slipping it back into her pocket during the day.

It was the next time around that Rainy had caught a glimpse of the intruder. She had been helping Ben cut and bind the wheat. It was hot for June, and she had removed the extra shirt she had put on in the cool of the early morning and left it folded on the edge of the field. Suddenly there was a flash in the corner of her eye, and she turned just in time to see something fall onto her shirt and a thin black girl with wild hair running for the trees. She must be from some house in the valley, Rainy had thought at once, bewildered. She must have stayed on with some family down in Serendipity after the war. And in the same instant she had wondered what such a person was doing up in their hills, where there had never been any slaves. Glancing over at Ben to make sure he was busy, she had walked toward the shining thing. She remembered now how it had looked at her feet, a solid silver bracelet with a flat green stone set in the center, and how it had felt when she had picked it up and slipped it over her wrist for an instant. Heavy. And how the green stone had looked, an oval, opaque and smooth, perfectly fitted into the silver. But she had taken it right off and hidden it as well, shoving it quickly down into her pocket, where it clicked against the necklace. She had known then she would have to tell Will. But she had put it off, keeping the strangeness of these occurrences to herself like a forbidden treasure.

That evening, Will had stayed out on the front porch of their house for a good long time, way after he usually retired for the night. Drifting sleeplessly, she heard him tuning his old Spanish guitar and, later still, heard him humming and wandering from tune to tune in his tenor voice. She had willed the singing to loosen the guilty knot in her stomach, and finally she had fallen asleep to the slow refrain of *I am a poor wayfaring stranger, a-trav'ling through this world of woe, and there's no sickness, toil, or danger in that bright land to which I go.*

Trembling, Rainy stepped out to the edge of the porch and looked down in the early morning light. A small red satin purse about the size of a folded handkerchief lay on the bottom step, tied closed with a ribbon of the same hue and sheen. She stepped down, leaned over, and slipped her fingers around the purse, feeling the smoothness of the satin and something inside, small and hard. She pulled on the ribbon and the bow slid open easily. She tipped the purse and a ring tumbled out into her cupped hand. Rainy caught her breath. The ring was gold, set with a bright clear stone that reflected the light every which way.

Now she knew with a guilty pang that she could no longer delay: this was too much, this was frightening. She would have to confess.

_____

Will

"You should have spoken to me about this before, Rainy," says Will in his most formal tone. He is holding himself straight like he does in church. They are sitting around the table, the three of them. At their eating places. But this is not a meal. They are staring at the three cold and elegant objects that Rainy has placed on the table, side by side. The silver medallion on its silver chain, the bracelet with its flat green stone, and the bright ring, all gleaming on the rough wood table. Ben extends a finger toward the ring, cautiously, as if it might bite.

"Are we rich?" he asks. "Could we sell this stuff?"

"Hush up, Ben," says Rainy. She is waiting for Will to continue.

But Will keeps silent, just goes on looking at the jewels. His face is thoughtful and sad. He seems to be lost in his silence. Finally he says, "I want to lock these up in the strongbox for the moment."

"I'll get it, Papa," says Ben. He crosses the room and lifts a dull gray metal box from the shelf over the stove, brings it back, and sets it down on the table in front of Will. Rainy and Ben know by heart what is in that box. Will keeps the deed to the farm in there, and a small framed picture of Ella, Ben's mama, who passed away when Ben was a baby. And a dried rose from Ella's wedding bouquet. And a rusty pistol from Will's great-grandfather, Samuel Barnes, who fought at King's Mountain back in Revolutionary times.

Reaching under his shirt, Will pulls up a small key that always hangs around his neck on a worn leather thong. He leans forward and unlocks the box. The hinges creak as he pulls up the lid. He waits, his hands resting on either side of the box. Understanding what Will expects, Rainy picks up each piece of jewelry, slips each one into the red purse, folds it over, and ties it closed with the ribbon. She lays the purse on top of the thick yellowing paper that is the deed to the land they live on. The shiny red satin looks strange there, out of place. Will closes the box at once with a firm hand, locks it. Without a word, Ben picks it up, crosses the room again, and puts it back on the shelf over the stove.

When Ben returns to the table, they just sit there, the three of them. No one says anything for a while. Will has closed his eyes, and his hands rest on his knees. He is leaning slightly forward, his tall, lanky body is quite still, and a mesh of graying hair has fallen in front of his eyes. Rainy thinks he might be praying. Or just listening to the world like he says he does sometimes, listening to the wind or the rain. Which he says is the same as praying. She and Ben wait for him to come back to them.

"Them jewels..." says Ben, when Will seems to notice them again.

"Those jewels," corrects Will in his normal teacher voice, pushing his hair back into place, a quick, familiar gesture of his long fingers.

"Yeah, well, those jewels, who would come up here and just throw 'em all on the ground? What sense is there in that? No sense at all. And what's a darky gal doing with jewels like that anyway? Can't be hers. And if she stole 'em, why come all the way up here just to throw 'em away?"

"Maybe it's something to do with me," Rainy says quietly.

"No, honey, no, no," says Will quickly. But Rainy hears a weariness in his voice that frightens her. She can feel her heart sinking, sinking.

About me, about me, she thinks to herself, whispering the words as she lies under her quilt that night. For who knows where I came from, she goes on silently. Slowly, as always, the "who knows" words won't stop and they turn into a song in her head, almost like it was Will himself singing out on the front porch. But this is not a song anyone can hear. It has no tune, it's like a wind that lives only in her mind. And she can't make it stop. *Who knows where I came from*, it goes, wailing and whirling along, *who knows who I may be? I was found on a rainy morning, I was found in the crook of a tree.*

But after the day of the red satin purse, the weeks went by uneventfully. Time almost seemed to slow down. The strange girl stopped coming, and Will kept silent about the whole business. And then the autumn was there, bringing rain and muddy roads and long walks to and from school for Rainy and Ben. And then the cold weather set in, bringing many days of no school, the season when they learned their lessons around the big table under Will's careful tutelage after the day's work. Rainy was a good reader, better than Ben even, in spite of being the younger child. Will gave her stories to read in the magazines he subscribed to. And some evenings after supper he would ask her to read a story aloud to him and Ben, saying that it was pleasant to hear her expressive voice. That she made the stories come alive. Ben always wanted stories from *Beadle's Dime Novels*, like "Steam Man of the Prairies," the one about a powerful locomotive built out of steel in the shape of a man. Or the ones about the river pirates. Or the Indian wars. And by and by winter closed in on them, and the snows came, and she tried, day after day, not to think about the jewels, to push them out of her memory. They were locked up in the strongbox, locked up in the dark, Rainy repeated to herself. Locked up in the dark, and that was that.

It was mostly in the winter that Will would tell Rainy's own special story, of how she came to them. Usually when the three of them were sitting together in front of the fireplace after supper. And so one snowy evening he began again, and Rainy felt sweet relief hearing the familiar words, like walking down to the river when spring came. Down to find old Robert Ray, see if he had any fish for sale. Or to look for scuppernongs.

And now the story came again in Will's slow voice, with the brightness of the apple tree in bloom on that rainy Sunday morning, just about a year before the war was over and when spring came really late, and how Ben wasn't more than knee high to a grasshopper back then and how they had suddenly heard a mewing sound from outside. And how he, Will, had stepped out onto the front porch and, my Lord, seeing a flash of color among the blossoms and hearing the mewing sound again and walking fast down to the tree and finding her there lying in the crook wrapped up tight in that big soft red blanket with just a few little raindrops on her cheeks. And how she had looked up at him with those pretty dark eyes and smiled, tiny as she was, and how he had picked her up and carried her back to the house.

There was always a pause in his telling at that point in the story. This time was no different. The concluding words came: "And you have been our own dear girl ever since."

"And then you named me," says Rainy, wanting it all, right to the last drop.

"Yes, we did indeed. We named you Blossom because of the flowering tree. But somehow it didn't stick, and we called you Rainy Day Baby for a while because you had come to us on that rainy day. And then just plain Rainy. Rainy Barnes."

Following the ritual, Will gave Rainy a big hug. But something was wrong. Because Ben did not pinch her leg as he usually did and there was no squealing and no ruckus with them chasing each other around the room and Will having to hush them up. Ben didn't make a move. Looking over at her brother, Rainy felt strange, almost as if she didn't know him anymore. The jewels hidden away in the dark, the necklace, the silver bracelet with its green stone, the shiny ring—these cold and mysterious intruders seemed to have pushed them out of childhood, as if the two of them had all of a sudden become too old for that kind of thing. Ben didn't look back at her. He just sat in front of the fireplace on a stool, his gangly body folded awkwardly, looking down at his hands, rubbing a callus. Outside, the snow was falling thick and fast, making a whispering against the shutters.

Rainy woke up, way past midnight, to a small creaking sound. She knew at once what it was. Opening her eyes from her bed behind the stove, she saw Will at the big table, standing over the open strongbox, slipping something into the pocket of his winter coat. He was dressed for the cold. He closed and locked the box, put it back on the shelf, and in a few swift steps was out the door and gone. She heard him riding away on Belle, and she listened to the muffled thumping of the mare's hooves on the snow-covered ground as it faded quickly away. Only the field cricket that had taken up refuge in the house went on singing its repetitious song. As if to comfort her. Whatever the jewels meant, whatever they were, wherever they came from, Will was doing something, he was taking care of the problem, just as he had always taken care of her.

She heard him return before dawn, but he just went straight out again with his rifle. When he came back, she had the coffee on, Ben was out chopping kindling, and Will had his easy smile, pulling a good-sized rabbit out of the hunting pouch. That evening they feasted on rabbit stew, and with the sweet pungent taste on her tongue Rainy felt her uneasiness lift. She felt safe again for the first time in weeks. All would be well. She and Ben would be brother and sister again. All would be like before.

Sleep came easily in her little alcove, the wood stove humming at her back, the snow piling up in drifts against the farmhouse under the winter wind. Soon it would be belly deep to a horse.

Marie Bijou

Down in Serendipity, down in the little valley town, the house full of summer air is ringing with vociferations from Marie Bijou. There is no stopping her. Gabrielle knows that when Marie Bijou is like this, when her voice begins to rise and fall and wail and shout, there is nothing to do but wait for the storm to end. The past, the present, all come together and are tossed around any which way in her orations.

"Ah, we were something in those days, is it not so? Not like now. We wanted for nothing! Monsieur Violet coming to the house for your pedicure. And Monsieur Valentin for the music lessons. And the sun shining in through the pink and yellow panes in the parlor, so beautiful. Not like now, *ma pauvre*. Not like in this godforsaken place. *Ah, Seigneur!* Why did I ever leave New Orleans? Why did I ever leave to follow your misty feet? I would rather still be a servant with your *maman* than here with you! *Malheur!* Look at this house! You have fine carpets, *ma pauvre*, but they lie on floors full of holes. And now he is gone, your husband. Gone these many months. I should have known,

I should have seen it coming, *imbécile que je suis*! I am leaving, *tu m'entends*? I am not waiting for you anymore. I am not staying another day in this place! I go home to my Pondy!"

"*Pour l'amour de Dieu*, Marie Bijou," pleads Gabrielle, "shut up, shut up with your jabbering."

"No, I don't shut up. I have not finished, not at all finished. We need to call the fool killer on you. Because I know now, I know now since today, that you have been sending my girl, my Rose, my own sweet child, with Pondichéry, my only child with my only love, you have been sending her since the springtime and all summer long, behind my back, you have been sending her with your precious jewels to throw them on the ground, on the ground like trash up there! First your silver necklace and then your *maman*'s jade bracelet and now, *nom de Dieu*, even the ring, the diamond ring! Rose, she has told me, she has told me all, and crying like a baby. You have pushed her to do this! Maybe she never found them, the child, *hein*? Maybe some stranger, some vagabond, he has picked them up and gone his way, *hein*? And what danger for my daughter from these wandering men. My daughter!"

Gabrielle lies back on the couch and closes her eyes. She answers in a low voice. "Stop talking nonsense. And nothing has happened to Rose. Be quiet, be quiet! And he will see the jewels because the child will show them to him and he will remember them from when they were around my neck and on my arm and on my finger. He will know I want to see her. He will bring her to me. Soon. I want the shadow off my face, Marie Bé. I want to see my child."

"Shadow, shadow, what do you know about shadow? I am

the one in shadow," mutters Marie Bijou. "Why did you call for me, why did you beg for me to come back? And why, *mon Dieu*, did I do it? Why did I not stay home? I have no life more, all these years, no joy more, no husband. I am nothing here. All this *par ta faute!*"

"By whose fault? By whose fault?" Gabrielle is shouting now, but her voice is full of grief. She rises quickly from the couch and runs upstairs, taking the steps two by two, feeling the tears burning, turning her back on the tempest.

"Don't follow me, Marie Bé," she calls behind her. "Leave me alone."

"Oh, I leave you, I leave you," comes the reply. "I leave you very soon for good."

Gabrielle lies down on her bed. Her eyes move as always to the windows, to the branches and the leaves outside provided by the mountain oaks that surround the house. As always she thinks that the trees are the best part about the place Jared had found for them. Back when he was ambitious. Back when he had dreams. Back before the war hollowed him out. He used to say that being in the bedroom was like being in a tree house. But Jared is gone now. Gone since the spring. Perhaps he has really been gone for years. Gone since he came back from the war no longer the same man. She closes her eyes, willing the present to disappear, praying for a few moments of peace, praying for peace until the bad comes back, as it always does, every time, like a tide.

Robert Ray

Robert Raymond Kincaid had always looked old to Rainy Barnes, but maybe he wasn't as old as all that. It was hard to tell with Robert Ray. For as long as she could remember, he had lived down by the fast-flowing Green River, about a quarter-mile from Papa Will's house and farm. He had built himself a kind of hut there, using an outcropping of rock as a back wall. It was a jumble of logs and beaver skins, nails, and rope, but was surprisingly dry inside when it rained and had an efficient smoke hole in the wintertime. Rainy never saw Robert Ray dressed in anything other than a patchwork of furs in the cold months and plain cotton shirts and overalls in the summer. Some people said he was part Cherokee for sure, but the red you could still see in his beard and hair seemed to indicate a different ancestry. The older people in the county said he had been married once to a Cherokee woman, and had gone away with her on the Trail of Tears. And that he had come back to North Carolina years and years later, alone. Some said it was all talk. And since Robert Ray was a loner and very close-mouthed about his past, people just left him to live his life as he saw fit. He was well known as a skilled fisherman—the best fly fisherman in the county and maybe in North Carolina, as Ben always claimed. Will would stop by Robert Ray's with Rainy and Ben from time to time to see if the old fellow had trout for sale, or one of his handmade lures. More often than not, though, Rainy knew it was just to check on him, to see if he was doing all right. Will was like that, and Rainy loved him for it.

"How old are you, Robert Ray?" Will asked one day for the umpteenth time when they were visiting.

"Hmmmm," came the usual answer. "Old enough."

"Caught anything today?"

"No. Wrong moon. Tomorrow should be better. Tomorrow should be good."

And they would go on sitting there for a long while in silence, sprawled comfortably along the riverbank. Sometimes there were scuppernongs and they would bite into the green and brown globes, exploding the sweet musky juices into their mouths and spitting out the bitter skin and seeds. Sometimes they would just listen to the water flowing by. Listen to the river talking to the trees, as Robert Ray liked to say. These quiet times with Robert Ray always meant that summer had come to stay.

Rainy liked to look at Robert Ray because of his eyes, which were a deep blue and sad. Looking into Robert Ray's eyes, she always felt an echo in herself; she recognized her own secret sadness in those eyes. And although he was a quiet man, Rainy always had the feeling that he had knowledge that was somehow kept from her. And that if she could just find a way, she could get him to talk. And tell her what she wanted to know. The thing she wanted to know without knowing what it was.

One day, late in the summer, when the red satin purse was still lying closed up in the strongbox, she had come upon Robert Ray in the woods. He was down on one knee, pulling a rabbit from one of his traps.

"Looks like you'll be having a good dinner tonight, Robert Ray," she remarked, just to get him talking.

"That's so."

But then the old man fell silent. So Rainy asked him to tell her the Cherokee hunting story, the one where the hunters and their dogs were after bear.

Robert Ray wasn't much for conversation, but he was always ready to tell a story from his time with the Cherokee. He laid the rabbit on the ground, sat back on his heels, and began. "Well, you see, there were four brothers, all great hunters. And they were after a giant bear who had been terrorizing the Cherokee villages. The bear climbed higher and higher into the mountains, but the brothers stayed after him. His trail was easy to follow because he was so big. And the hunters had a little tracker dog who stayed close behind the bear, yapping at his heels. Up and up the mountain they went, higher and higher. They could hear the little dog yapping, but they couldn't seem to catch up to the bear. Finally, when the hunters thought they could climb no more, they came upon the bear at last. There he was, a gigantic beast, standing on his hind legs, growling and showing his teeth and swiping at the little dog with his huge front paw that had claws as long as your arm. When the bear saw the hunters he ran straight at them. It was a horrible sight. But the best hunter of the four brothers stood his ground and thrust his spear right through the heart of the great bear and killed him dead right there and then. Well, the four brothers were really proud and happy. They all felt like heroes. They cut up the bear and built a fire and began to feast. The bear grease made sparks as it dripped into the fire. And that roasted bear meat was delicious, and the brothers ate and ate until they were full. But then, suddenly, one of the brothers noticed little tiny lights in the dark way far below his feet. And the brothers saw that they were not on a mountaintop at all. The magical giant bear had led them up a strange trail right into the world of the sky. At that instant the big pile of bear bones began to jiggle and jump and come together and the bear came back to life. And the hunters grabbed their spears and began chasing the bear all over again across the sky with the little dog running ahead of them. And if you look, you can still see them all up there, twinkling away," concluded Robert Ray. "White folks call it the Big Dipper."

"That's my favorite story," said Rainy. "Would you tell me another one? Tell me about the river monster."

But the old man had stopped talking. He remained quite motionless, still sitting on his heels, seemingly lost in thought.

Rainy reached out and shook his arm.

"Robert Ray?"

No answer. She shook his arm again.

"Robert Ray?"

He turned his head, their eyes met, and Rainy realized that he had heard her perfectly.

"You know real things too, don't you?" said Rainy. "Not just stories." She was caught now in the old man's sad blue gaze. Her heart was beating fast.

"What things, little one?"

"I mean, you know about things around here, around this county, things that happened way back before I was born."

"What gives you that idea?"

"I don't know. I just have it. Is it true nobody knows where I came from?"

"Nobody who?"

"Will. Papa Will. And Ben."

Robert Ray rose to one knee again like he was getting ready to leave. He lifted the limp rabbit from the ground and slid it into a leather pouch he wore slung over one shoulder. He picked up a dry pine branch and began digging a kind of channel in the earth. "I mind my own business."

Rainy knew she had crossed a border and was entering unknown country. She was a little frightened, yet she went on. "I mean Papa Will always says he never could find out anything about me. Not a thing. Now what do you think about that?"

Robert Ray did not answer and began to dig harder and to grumble one of his songs that sounded like Indian chanting. Rainy knew these songs were something from his long-ago days with the Cherokee. And when he started grumbling and humming like that, Rainy knew there wouldn't be another word.

But then Robert Ray turned to her suddenly and spoke again in a rough voice. She had never heard him speak so roughly. His eyes had turned hard, and his voice was almost a growl. "Best you let sleeping dogs lie, my girl. You go on home now. You go on home." And he rose to his feet and walked away, back toward the river.

Because hadn't he seen the Creole woman in the hour before dawn scuffling over the log bridge with her bundle, scuffling over the bridge a ways up from where he was setting his traps? Yes, he had seen her with his own eyes, all those years ago, that tall mulatto woman in a big hurry, carrying something up the path to Will Barnes's cabin. A something that he knew right off what it was.

Rainy

After her talk with Robert Ray, Rainy felt very strange for a few days, like her heart was a pond frozen over in the dead of winter. But then she began to feel like something inside her was melting. And when the thing felt like a tear just about to fall, she began to walk up to the headwaters of the Green on Sunday afternoons, to the place where the wealthier families from the valley would go during the hottest months.

Creeping through the trees, during the last summer days, she watches them walking to and fro, the people who still live in the bigger houses down in Serendipity, those who are still hanging on down in the dying town, as Will always calls it. "A dying town. Best they should all just clear out and never come back." Will never goes down there, never goes to the church there, keeps away from the place like it had the plague. This makes Rainy all the more curious about the matronly ladies she sees up here, stepping along together arm in arm under the trees. And the men who gather in groups, speaking in low voices like lazy thunder from far away. From time to time, younger couples drive up in a rattling buggy with their children. Little girls in white lace dresses and button-up boots, little boys in trousers and jackets. Some days she can hear the tinny strains of an old piano coming from the open windows of a summerhouse, set further back under the pines, its white paint cracked and peeling. Sometimes she creeps closer and observes the people as they seat themselves just outside the decrepit house around rusty metal tables under the trees, a few men and women seated together now, laughing and talking and drinking the spring water in glass mugs that a Negro waiter brings out on a tray. And also a few children playing tag and counting out in their high voices to see who would be it.

"Wire briar, limber lock,
three geese in a flock.
One flew east and one flew west
and one flew over the cuckoo's nest."

The war had happened, and now the valley town is dying, fields lying fallow, businesses disappeared, but these people, Rainy knows, are trying to live just like they did before, just as if there had been no war at all. Like playing pretend the way she does with Ben sometimes. Let's pretend we're pirates, let's pretend we're medieval knights. But there had been a war, of course, hadn't there, because, as she knows each time the idea looms in her mind, bringing a thrill of fear, hadn't she somehow come into being because of this war?

One evening, summer seems to be ending. The leaves in the lower forest have begun to turn yellow and red, and there is a chill in the air. Rainy is sitting in front of the fire turning the pages of an old magazine of Will's. She looks at the date on the yellowing cover. It reads *June 4, 1864.* That's over ten years ago, she thinks. It's my age. The magazine is as old as I am. She reads the caption printed under a picture, a black-and-white engraving. It says *Our wounded escaping from the fires in the Wilderness.* The picture shows two soldiers carrying a companion on a makeshift stretcher, the body humped down and hidden inside a sheet tied between two poles. They are Yankee soldiers in the picture, and they are moving through a burning forest, flames licking at their heels, cinders falling from the trees.

"What was the Wilderness?" she asks.

Will looks up from his book. Ben turns away from his homework at the table.

"A terrible battle during the war," says Will. "Up in Virginia. Terrible. A madness. Thousands and thousands of men died there, North and South alike." He goes back to his book. Without looking up again, he adds, as he almost always does when talking about the war, "The breaking away from the Union was a tragic mistake. And now we pay the price."

Rainy keeps quiet because if Will gets going about the Yankee marauders and the price that is being paid, he will not stop for a long time and she has heard it all over and over. And how he and Robert Ray picked off a few with their hunting rifles just to keep them out of their mountains. No, what she wonders about is the war. The real war with the big battles and the shooting and the cannons and the wounded and the dying. What was that like? She runs her fingers over the picture, over the Yankee soldiers' boots, over their hands gripping the poles, over the invisible body hanging heavy in the sheet, over the embers falling from the burning trees. Yes, she is certain that somehow, somehow, it is this war that made her.

Far to the north of Rainy, up in Virginia, at the place called the Wilderness, the underbrush has grown back riotously, hiding the treacherous, uneven ground. The fires from the old battle have made the vegetation stronger, the trees that survived the burning are taller and more vigorous. Hidden under the convulsive growth lie water bottles, rusting rifles, scattered shells, and unburied bones.

Gabrielle

Waking in the middle of the summer night from a bad dream, Gabrielle calls out for Marie Bé. The Creole comes to her, but to comfort, not to scold. Marie Bé holds her, rocking her wordlessly. "I was dying, Marie Bé," Gabrielle sobs. "I was disappearing into the ground like water."

"You here, *ma chérie*," Marie Bijou croons to her. "You here, you here. *Tu ne vas pas mourir.* You don't die, silly girl. You right here. Stop your crying now, *tout doux, tout doux.* Sleep, *dors, dors,* sleep."

"Don't leave me, Marie Bé," she whispers. "Don't leave me all alone."

"I don't leave you, *ma chérie*," comes the answer. "You sleep now, you sleep, *petite soeur.*"

She drifts off for a while, but awakens again soon, alone once more in the room, feeling all over again the shock that Jared is gone. Her husband has left her, has disappeared, taking only his battered leather suitcase, some shirts and trousers, a few law books, a few back issues of his agricultural journals. It is as if he had never returned from the war, thin, gaunt, bearded, the ironic smile erased from his lips and all the lighthearted banter too. In place of her young husband she had found herself married to a glum and moody man with a limp who studied his law books and journals late into the night and seemed to have no time for anything but worry. And now. Now it is as if he had never come back at all, as if the terror of his return had never existed, nor the devouring fear which had made her do the awful thing.

How had they lived together for all those years since the end of the war, she wondered. Sometimes they would find each other again, during certain drowsy afternoons, lying in the bed together with the summer leaves rustling outside the open windows and a little breeze blowing over them. And afterwards they would listen to little Rose down in the kitchen singing, "Pie dough, pie dough, we make pie dough," and Marie Bé's melodious answer, "*Oui, ma chérie*, pie dough, *oui, mon petit chou*, we make pie dough."

But there had been no children. And one evening Jared had come back from one of his long rides in the woods with a dark look in his eyes. At the dinner table he broke the silence that had grown between them. The sound of his voice made her jump.

"My horse nearly threw me today. Perhaps you would like to know why?"

"Why is that?" she had asked, somewhat warily.

"I ran across a vision, my dear. I never saw such a creature. A little girl. Like a forest sprite or a nymph. She could not have been more than ten years old. She was wearing overalls like a farmer, but what a beauty, with a long auburn braid hanging down her back. And carrying a little bow with a *parflèche* of arrows slung over her shoulder. She appeared so suddenly my horse reared up. And by the time I had recovered my balance she had fled like lightning. Just disappeared in an instant, as if by magic."

Gabrielle said nothing for a moment, but she could feel her husband waiting for a reply. Gathering her strength she remarked, "That could be William Barnes's child. He's an upland farmer. A widower. He has a big farm up there. He owns the land. Mr. Barnes has a son as well, I believe."

"You seem to know a great deal about these mountain people, my dear."

"Oh, you hear these things around town, at the store. People talk to pass the time. Maybe Marie Bé told me."

"Ah, yes, Marie Bé," he said. And got up from the table with his usual curt phrase: "If you will excuse me, I have work."

She was tempted to say, Work for what? There is no work anymore. There is nothing, nothing, nothing. She wanted to speak up, to shout, to give up her burden. But she held her tongue. Marie Bé came in to clear the table and gave her a hard look.

But then, a few days later, she told him. On another one of those drowsy afternoons, the words came out at last.

"Jared, I have a child." He turned his head slowly to look at her, his face registering no surprise, only his dark eyes turning darker. "She was born during the war. It's that little girl you saw up in the pines."

Jared went on looking at her for a while. Finally he said, "I think I have known for a long time. I have only been waiting for you to say it."

He got up then without asking another question and went out of the room. She heard him going down the stairs, his footsteps heavy and slow. And the next morning, he was gone. It was spring and he was gone.

Gabrielle turns in the bed to find Marie Bé standing silently before her. She waits for an outburst, a reproach, but none comes. Marie Bé just keeps on staring at her in the early morning light.

"*Eh bien, qu'est-ce qu'il y a?* What is it?" says Gabrielle at last.

Marie Bijou sits down on the edge of the bed, like in the old days at home in New Orleans when they were children, plotting something together. She takes Gabrielle's hand.

"*Ma* Gaby," she says, "*écoute-moi bien,* listen to me. I am very quiet now, I am peaceful and you will listen to my words, which are words of wisdom. We must go home. I cannot stay here anymore. We must go back to New Orleans. There is nothing here anymore. Monsieur Jared, he is not coming back. He will never come back. Not to you and not to this place."

"How do you know that? You don't know that." Gabrielle's voice has risen, it trembles.

"Hush, hush. I have seen him. He woke me in the night, that night when he went away. He said, 'Marie Bijou, I have to leave this place.'"

"He came to you? He came to you? And not to me?"

"This was his way. And so I said, *Oui, monsieur.* I know."

"He came to you and not to me. Not even a letter, nothing. And you never told me this. Why? Why?"

"Listen to me. Here are his words. 'I have to go away,' he said, 'it is too hard for me here, too much pain. You take my wife home to her *maman*, you take her back to New Orleans with Rose and Joseph. You take her home for good. No more trips up and down, no more coming and going. This is the end. I am selling this house. I have written to my aunt in Raleigh to do the papers.'"

Marie Bé pauses. She begins rubbing Gabrielle's fingers. Gently, persuasively. "So," she goes on. "Do you understand? *Tu m'entends, ma chérie?* Do you hear what I am saying?"

Gabrielle looks up into Marie Bé's familiar face, the smooth brown skin, the almond eyes, the high cheekbones, the finely drawn lips, and she hangs on to the sight as her tears begin to flow. Her grip tightens on Marie Bé's hand. She feels she has lost her voice.

"I can't go yet, Marie Bé," she whispers. "Not yet. You go first, you and Rose. Let Joseph stay on for just a few more weeks to help me out. And then he and I will come home."

"Jojo!" Marie Bé's voice rises. "You know my Pondy is waiting for him. He needs him for work, for the furniture making. Jojo, he is wasting away down here. There are no more clients for cupboards and tables like before. *Non, chérie*, we got to go home, all of us together. Before the summer ends. Joseph and Rose and me to Pondy, you to your *maman*."

Gabrielle turns her face away. "You know very well I cannot go."

Marie Bé tightens her grip on Gabrielle's hand. "Don't hope in that direction, *petite*. It is too late for that. *Bien trop tard.* Give it up. Let it go. The child doesn't even know you. And

Monsieur Will, he will never give her up."

Gabrielle tears her fingers from Marie Bé's grasp and runs to the window in her bare feet, tears in her throat.

"And by your fault, by your fault!" she cries out. "You made me do it! You pestered me and pestered me till I gave in."

Marie Bé falls silent.

"Just a few more weeks," says Gabrielle in a quieter voice. "You and Rose go on home. You write to Pondichéry, he will come for you. I know you are longing to see him, *n'est-ce pas?* Go, go, go write your letter. I will be fine."

The image of her husband has caused Marie Bé to rise and to step away as if Pondy were already downstairs at the front door.

But before going out of the room, she stares hard at Gabrielle and whispers, "You are mad, and me, you will drive me mad!" Adding loudly, as she clumps down the stairs, "And your *maman*, how will I tell her?"

That evening, they cook together wordlessly, Marie Bé making the corn bread while Gabrielle fries the tomatoes and boils the peas. Joseph hangs around in the doorway watching them, waiting for a word from either one. When the food is ready, with a quick "*Je vous laisse*" he takes his supper out to the barn, where he sleeps on a mattress among his tools and boards.

In the dining room, Gabrielle and Marie Bé eat slowly, heads bowed over their plates, sitting together again like when they were children, now that Jared is gone. Rose watches them between bites, hoping for a release from disgrace.

"We got to leave," says Marie Bé in her stubborn voice as she gathers up the empty plates.

"Oh, don't start up again." Gabrielle sighs. "Let's talk about something else."

"*Non, non, et non!*" Marie Bé is almost shouting. "You are only trying to change the subject, and there is only one, one, one subject we need to talk about."

"Oh please, Marie Bé, do let's keep quiet for a while. Let's remember how Pondy used to watch over us in the old days. Let's talk about when we would slip away from Maman at the Mardi Gras parades. Please. Remember how we didn't even know he was there, but he always was. Remember how he would hide so we could feel daring and have our fun. But he was always just a few steps behind us, ready to jump out if we ran into trouble."

Marie Bijou said nothing, drawn in against her will. Gabrielle, sensing victory, went on in a low voice. "Remember when we were butterfly and bee? And that *saleté*, that river rat, that boatman thief who tried to grab your purse? Remember when he pulled his knife to frighten you? There was Pondy, *ting! bing!* like he had jumped up out of the ground, like a jack-in-the-box, and that fool's nose was broken in half a tick. And how he ran!"

"My Pondy," murmured Marie Bé. "He loved me then already, but I was too silly to see, too young, *trop bête!* We had life in those days, *hein?* Ha! Ha! Remember the Mardi Gras parade when they all turned to look as we walked by. What a sight we were, you the butterfly and me the bee, and our silk dresses and our beautiful wings and the little shiny sequins on our shoes, ah, so bright! And once they applauded and cheered even, remember the cheering? How we curtsied, how we danced. Right in the street. We had life, we had life!"

"Tell more, tell more stories!" says Rose, feeling herself released from her mother's disapproval, relieved by the familiar sounds of conversation between the two women.

But Marie Bé snaps at her daughter. "You are disgraced! You have no say."

"Not my fault," mumbles Rose, swinging her legs under the chair, scuffing her feet on the floorboards. "Madame Gaby, she made me go."

"Madame Gaby, Madame Gaby, what is this? You are a free person of color, a free person of *La Nouvelle-Orléans*. You learn first some sense. And if something is not right, *nom de Dieu*, by God, you learn to say no."

Gabrielle says nothing, eager for peace, and as the sun goes down, with Rose listening to them quietly, they get back to talking in the old way and she and Marie Bé sit in the half-light of the shabby dining room, recalling the past until darkness falls and they have to light a lamp. Later, after the dishwashing in the back kitchen, Marie Bé and Rose retire to their sleeping places in the downstairs bedroom and Gabrielle goes up to hers. The leaves of the oaks outside the open windows are turning to silver in the moonlight. She pushes her bare feet up into the dark. They make her think of two slender trees swaying. What if she could somehow turn into a tree like the nymph, Daphne, in the Greek legend? She had always been taken with the story. Ever since she was a child looking into the big book, sitting on her father's lap, seeing the pictures, the detailed black-and-white engravings, one after the other as he turned the heavy pages with his long and graceful fingers. There is the nymph, pursued by the god, Apollo. She runs from him like the wind, yet she cannot escape, feels him close behind her, his hot breath on her neck. Now she prays to the river god, her father, to save her, save her, and suddenly her racing feet are pulled down into the earth and become roots and in the same instant her arms fly up and turn into branches. That would take the pain away, yes, thought Gabrielle. If I could just be a tree swaying in the wind and the child would come and play in my shade.

Rose

All the days have become strange. They make her feel jittery inside. And sad. And dark. And her *maman* and Madame Gaby are always looking like they are angry with each other. It's not like when she and Maman used to sing "Pie dough, pie dough" when she was little, kneading and pressing, kneading and pressing, side by side in the warm kitchen. Maman and Madame Gaby, they don't even have the same voices anymore. And she hates the way they stop talking when she comes into a room. She knows very well that it all has to do with Monsieur Jared going away in the spring without a word. So why do they stop talking like that? Do they think she has no eyes to see? Do they think she is still a baby? Do they think she did not notice, as she got older, how his bad leg from the war began to drag more and more? And how quiet he had become. Sort of like he had been thrown out into the dark like a stray cat. He was all sad and quiet and out in the dark. Kept out of the secret, the secret shared by her *maman* and Madame Gaby. The thing they won't tell her either. Something up at that farm, that farm up the mountain path.

But now that he's gone, it's worse. Maman and Madame Gaby hardly ever play music anymore like they used to. It's like they can't find the time or they just don't want to do it anymore. No more piano, no more violin. She misses it. When they played, it was joyful, as if the piano and the violin were running after each other, leaping and rolling, coming together and separating, sometimes echoing each other, slowly, slowly, and then the piano would sound like it was tiptoeing under the violin, which seemed to be weeping over some terrible grief, but then the piano would change and seem to be saying, *I am here, I am here*, and the violin with a long, long tone would seem to answer, *Yes, I am here too, I know, we are one*, and the music would whirl away, dizzyingly fast. And the two of them would go on playing, on and on as the sun sank lower, finally fading out with a few words of laughter and then stopping altogether at nightfall, abandoning the air to the crickets singing in the grass. On some evenings, though, they would just sing, the simple old rounds from New Orleans, and she and even Jojo would come join in for "Frère Jacques" so they would have their four voices blending and rising and falling. But all of this is gone, as if making music had become an impossible something from the past. And it gives her the jittery, jumpy feeling like she wants to be away from this place. And her *maman* keeps telling her they are going soon, but she hasn't even begun to pack the trunk. She just keeps arguing with Madame Gaby, keeps on saying, We got to go. But they don't go.

She knows it has to do with Madame Gaby pushing the candy and the pennies and the lace into her hand and looking so frightened and fierce. Please, please, she would say. One last time. *Pour moi, Rose, pour moi.* Do this for me. You remember the path. It will take you straight up there, over the log bridge straight on up to the farm. You go early, you don't tell Marie Bé. You don't throw this on the ground, she had said, handing her a little red satin purse. You leave it at the house up there, you leave it on the front steps. It's our secret, *n'est-ce pas?*

Jared

Jared Balfour leans back in the swaying coach, traveling west, the Mississippi River behind him already for many days. He is free, his feet are free inside his boots, his eyes are free to look wherever he wishes them to look. The coach heaves and jolts, the horses at a full gallop. Once again the realization washes over him: he has really gone away, he has really left her, he is on his way to somewhere, on his way to God knows where, but on his way. His way. Sometimes he has guilty thoughts of Gabrielle. And he remembers with a twinge of regret the feel of her small feet on his when she was curled up in the bed, the touch of those little feet on his when they slept back to back. But today he is not sorry. He can breathe. It seems he has not breathed in this way for many years. He is enjoying these moments of elation, even the dusty air as he draws it into his lungs. Once, in a hotel in St. Louis, he had had a dream of the beautiful child glimpsed so briefly up in the woods back home. The child with something about the turn of her shoulders and the curve of her cheek and the quick glance from her dark eyes that had made his heart sink. She was telling him to go in her shy way. Go, sir, she had said in the dream, although he could not hear her voice. Go, sir, you must go. You are like a big rock blocking the path. You are a dam blocking the river. And then she had run away. And then he had been in a fast-flowing river, fighting the current, trying not to drown.

The coach rumbles on. Jared shifts in his seat, trying to find a position of less discomfort.

"*Oh, what was your name in the States?*" went the California gold rush song, drifting, unbidden, through his head. Where had he heard it? Somewhere during the war?

> *"Oh, what was your name in the States?*
> *Thompson or Johnson or Bates?*
> *Did you murder your wife and fly for your life?*
> *Oh, what was your name in the States?"*

Jared closes his eyes, the feeling of elation recedes, and he finally gives in to the cursing of his grinding soul and he damns her to hell once more, damns her eyes, her mouth, her pretty little breasts, her smell, her tangled hair all perfume, her voice, her lost looks, her stillness, her secrets, her quicksilver ways. He rubs his beard and tastes the dust on his tongue and damns her to hell all over again in the shaking, rumbling coach. He suppresses the violent sob in his throat. And finally, his mind fleeing the bitter complaint, his body exhausted from too little sleep, he fades into unconsciousness.

When he opens his eyes once more, a stout black woman in elegant mourning dress has changed places in the coach and moved to the seat opposite him. A small boy nestles in the crook of her arm. The boy is looking at him with undisguised curiosity. The woman notices this and chides her son. "Don't stare, James, it's not polite."

The boy squirms, embarrassed, and lowers his gaze.

"Listen to that wind," says a thin, dark-suited gentleman on Jared's right, clutching his briefcase, which Jared knows, from the man's showing of its contents during the last stop at a way station, is full of cheap jewelry and lace. Just as he knows the woman in mourning is the widow of a Yankee soldier from a Negro regiment. The coach bumps and sways along under the rising wind. There is a lingering smell of sweat and meat pies from the last meal.

An hour later the coach pulls up in front of a long, low building. The passengers pile out, the wind pushes at their backs, whistling from across the flat plain. Lightning flashes from the horizon and the sky is black. The travelers clump up the wooden steps, across the wide boards of the porch and into the long, narrow room. A fire flickers and crackles from the fireplace at the far end. A sturdy young woman is greeting the passengers one by one as they enter. She has a wide face with high cheekbones and pale blue eyes, and wears a plain dark blue dress and apron.

"Good evening, evening, evening all, I'm Alma Westerwald, yes, yes, I am the station master, I myself, don't be surprised. Come on in, come on in, coats on the hooks please. Welcome, welcome, supper's just about ready." Jared finds his right hand clasped in a firm grip. It is a hard-working hand, yet gentle somehow. "Come on in and make yourself to home."

She has a distinct accent. German, he guesses, noticing also the thick blond braid coiled and pinned around her head.

As the travelers seat themselves around a wooden table, Alma Westerwald is lighting the candles in their holders along the wall. An oil lamp suspended from a hook in the ceiling already spreads its glow over the table. There is a heavy scraping of chairs as the hungry people take their places.

The driver of the coach, a man obviously at home at the way station, lifts a large cast-iron kettle from the woodstove and sets it down on a flat stone in the middle of the table. Armed with a ladle, Alma Westerwald begins to serve from the steaming kettle. "Hand me your plates now," she calls. "Chicken and dumplings, I hope you will like it."

"Best stop on the westward line, folks," says the driver. "No boiled beans at Alma's table. There's no better cook for a thousand miles around. "

"You hush up, Pete," says Alma. "Help with the plates."

The food is good, simple and hot. Jared savors the tender chicken, the slightly sweet dumplings, the thick gravy. He drinks some water from his earthenware mug. But suddenly his heart goes tight, he feels breathless, no, worse, he is suffocating, the fear grips his chest. What in God's name am I doing here? What will become of her? To what mediocre destiny will she go? He closes his eyes, and slowly the feeling fades. He takes shelter in the thought that he has provided for her, that a good part of the money from the sale of the house will go to her. And that she will surely go home. Yes, surely go home to her mother, back to the big house on Esplanade. He goes on eating in small bites, mechanically, back bent, eyes lowered, barely noticing the chatter around him as the food begins to loosen people's tongues. He feels like a ghost. He should have died at the Wilderness. He should have bled to death on the burning ground. Perhaps he did die there, and all that has happened since then is nothing but a dream. And even this, the long table, the rough-hewn floorboards, the rising wind outside, the fire crackling away, perhaps this also is nothing but a dream.

"Your plate, sir?" Alma Westerwald is speaking to him.

He hands her his empty plate. "I beg your pardon," he mumbles.

Now people are getting up from their chairs and Alma Westerwald is calling out more orders. "The coach cannot go on in this weather. You will have to sleep here as best you can. Some to the coach, some to the barn, bedroom back this way for the lady and her boy."

Jared does not retire to the barn or to the coach with the other men. He walks toward the fireplace, feeling the old pain in his hip, and lowers his body into a rocking chair in front of the fire. The satiny black lady rustles past him with her sleeping son in her arms. Jared leans forward, elbows on his knees, and watches the embers.

Suddenly he senses a presence, turns and sees that Alma Westerwald is standing just a few steps behind his chair. He encounters the frank blue gaze. It seems to carry a meaning. Her eyes are saying that there is an order to the world, that the work of the day is done, that it is time for sleep. Some light wisps from her bun have fallen, curling around her face.

"Perhaps, sir, you will prefer to remain here to sleep?" she asks bluntly.

Jared remembers the warm grip of her hand, its curious gentleness.

"Please, yes, if it is not too much trouble."

"Of course, of course, I will bring right away something for the night."

A few moments and she is handing him a thick folded blanket.

"You are of the South?" she asks. The wide-set eyes are grave, curious.

"Yes, that I am," he answers. "Or was. Or am."

"You go where?"

Jared laughs and looks back up at her again.

"Well, my dear lady, I am not quite sure about that," he answers, surprised by the unaccustomed feeling of a smile playing around his lips. "Not quite sure about that at all. Perhaps you have a suggestion?"

"It is not my business," she answers evenly. "I only ask, for I see many like you. The war has made them poor. They look for a new life. Perhaps this is your case."

"The war, the war..." His voice trails off and his eyes wander back to the dying fire. "Yes, the war has made me poor indeed."

"Where do you fight in this war?"

"Oh, different places. I was at the Wilderness. That was the worst time I went through."

"And in this Wilderness place, have you killed many of those you call damnyankees?"

"That is hard to say. I fired, yes, I shot my rifle. But at the Wilderness you could not see what you were firing at."

"And why for is that, sir?"

Jared pauses and for a while he cannot find any words. Because there aren't any. Finally he gives up and says, "Too many trees. And smoke and fire. If hell were a forest, it would be like that place."

Alma Westerwald pulls a chair out of the shadows and sits down next to Jared. She waits, saying nothing. He feels no urgency in her. He watches the embers' slow glowing.

"I do know I killed one man for sure," he says after a while. "I had gotten separated from my battalion and I sort of stumbled into a clearing and there was a Yank over on the other side, just leaning against a tree. And the tree was all covered with flowers, a dogwood in full bloom. Like bloody flowers in hell, if you will pardon my language. And then the fellow made a move and I shot him and he just kind of slid to the ground. It was a clean shot to the heart. When I got to him he was dead for sure. He already had a head wound. I think maybe I just put him out of his misery. I hope so."

Jared pauses for a long time before going on. When he speaks again, his voice is unsteady.

"I went through his pockets and then I took his boots. They were almost new and mine were falling apart. They were just my size too." He glances over at Alma Westerwald, putting a hard glint in his eyes and a tight smile on his lips. "A stroke of luck, if you like."

Alma Westerwald gets up and stirs the fire with a poker and, taking a small log from the pile to the side of the fireplace, throws it on with a practiced gesture. The flames leap up at once around the dry wood.

Sitting down again and wiping her hands on her apron, she says, "This, all this, all this war from so long ago, this is part of your sadness, but I am thinking it is not everything. This is not what makes you walk with your back bent like an old man."

Jared turns his head once more toward the wide-set blue eyes and wonders, crazily, if he could lose himself there, drown, sink, dissolve.

"Quite right, madame," he replies. "You are a perspicacious lady indeed."

"I know not that word, sir," she answers briskly, "but I have eyes to see and a heart to feel. You sleep now. It is late."

She is gone. Jared rolls up in the blanket and stretches out on the floorboards before the fire. He closes his eyes, sees the westward road again. Suddenly he remembers the grandfather clock and the chest of drawers. They had been lying on the side of the road, tipped over, broken, abandoned by some overburdened travelers years before. He had glanced at them as the coach rumbled past, remarking their surfaces, surely once dark and shiny, now split and whitened and worn by the wind and the rain. He had imagined the scene as it might have happened. He had conjured up shadowy figures and a man's rough voice: "We can't carry these any further, Mother, we got to lighten the load." And then a woman's heavy sigh. Sometimes, too, he would spot a few graves along the road, their wooden crosses heaving this way and that. And always the rumbling and groaning of the wheels carrying him further and further west.

An hour later, the storm is full upon the way station, the thunder makes the glass in the windows rattle. Jared, the blanket pulled up tightly around his shoulders, watches the embers dying down until the storm subsides. Then the rain comes, heavy, pounding on the roof and on the ground all around, and with the rain comes sleep.

Pondichéry

Marie Bijou plays the going-home scenes once again in her head. But this time is different. Pondy is coming to fetch her and he is coming soon. If the date in his last letter is correct, he will arrive tomorrow. She rubs the clothes along the tin ridges of the washboard and plunges them back down into the soapy water in the tub. She chants in her head as she works. Yes, yes, yes. She conjures up the sight of her mother's house, the crape myrtle with its pink blossoms beside the doorstep, the high picket fence, the sloping roof, the garden with its fruit trees. Her house now. Her house to go home to. Her house waiting. Pondy will have waxed the floors and prepared their beds and tended the garden. Suddenly she can hear the street calls from the market, clear as a bell. *Waaaatermelon. Cantaloupe, cantaloupe, smell 'em, smell 'em. Sand! Want saaand! Sand your kitchen, sand your doors, sand your doorstep, sand your floors! Want saaaandeeee!*

She scrubs and rubs and rinses and scrubs again. Yes, yes, yes, at last yes. A big weight is lifting from her heart. In spite of Gabrielle. No more thinking about Gabrielle. No, no, no. She scrubs fiercely. Her exile is coming to an end. She has written to Pondy. The going-home time is at hand.

The next morning, she stands waiting by the road that passes in front of their house in Serendipity. The day announced in his letter has come. The shroud of trees is behind her and she is watching for him. And then he appears, only small, way down at the other end, driving a wagon pulled by two horses. But soon she can hear the rattling of the wagon and then she sees him clearly, his head and shoulders against the sky with the reins in his hands. He is wearing a red shirt and she runs, runs, runs as fast as she can run toward that moving wagon and there he is looking down at her as her breath comes fast. A few strands of white in his hair but the same good eyes, and he reins in the team and jumps down to her and his arms go around her and they have their world again.

When they drive away the next day, Gabrielle stays inside the house, does not come out to wave. Only Joseph stands there like a lone sentry in front of the trees. As they rattle away in the wagon, Rose points up at the sky and cries, "Look, the pigeons flying south! Going home like us." And she answers her daughter, saying, "Yes, *merci mon Dieu*, we go home."

The first night on the road, they sleep in the wagon because they are not yet at the train station. They have nothing but a canvas roof over their heads on that first night on the road. And she and Pondy lie together, face to face under this canvas roof, their arms around each other, their knees touching, and Rose is curled up at their feet. And Pondy kisses her forehead and strokes her cheek. And then he whispers in her ear, slowly, so she will feel the weight of what he has to say, although he has said it many times before in his badly written letters. But now he says it in his real voice. "You must not call me Pondichéry anymore. No one calls me that now back home. My name has changed, and this name is now painted on my shop. It says Pierre Lebois, *menuisier*, carpenter. Do you understand me, *ma chérie*? Do you understand me, my little bee?"

She does not answer right away, but then she whispers back to him, "Pierre, Pierre Lebois. A good name. I will learn to say it."

Rainy

Will is telling a Bible story to Rainy and Ben. But he is not reading it straight out of the book. Mostly he tells them in his own words. And Rainy suspects him of making some things up as he goes along. But this is what makes the stories so good to listen to. Sort of like seeing young green branches on a big old tree. When he begins the story of baby Moses in Egypt, she always finds herself listening more intently. Tonight, as Will speaks, she can picture everything he is telling very clearly. First the Hebrew woman, the mother, as Will describes her, walking quickly and oh so quietly through the dark village streets, holding a wicker basket close to her breast. She hurries on; she must not be seen, especially not by the soldiers. The basket of river reeds in her arms has been made waterproof with a thick layer of pitch and grease. Small sounds come from the basket. Because inside it is a little baby boy. The woman's own child. Now she is crossing a field of wheat, back bent, head down, almost running, keeping to a narrow path. Lifting her head from time to time, she can see the brightness of the great river

Nile moving under the stars. She reaches the edge of the water and stops to catch her breath. The earth is wet under her bare feet. Now she is slipping through the reeds at the edge of the water, moving forward until the water is up to her knees, up to her waist. She finds a place among the reeds, far enough from the shore to be a hiding place but where the current is not yet strong enough to pull the basket out into the stream. The child murmurs, sleeps. His belly is full; she has nursed him well. She will come back to nurse him again. Here in the hiding place. She kisses his soft forehead and lays the basket down between the reeds. Here he will be safe, she hopes, from the soldiers. Those who are sent out every day by Pharaoh to take the boy babies born to the Hebrew slaves and drown them in the Nile.

Soldiers, soldiers, always soldiers. Were they anything like the Yankees at the Wilderness, Rainy wonders. No, she thinks. No, more like the ones that Robert Ray sometimes talks about when his words slow down and he smells like whiskey. Those who drove him and his Cherokee family away from their home, those who caused his wife and children to die of hunger and cold, far from home. The wife, the boy, the girl.

Will's voice comes back to her. These Pharaoh soldiers, he is saying, these Pharaoh soldiers have been sent to kill the boy babies, only the boys. They have been ordered to allow the girl babies to live. Because Pharaoh wants the little girls to grow up and marry Egyptians and have Egyptian children. So that, after a time, there will be no more of these foreign Hebrews who have become so numerous in the land of Egypt. But, says Will after a significant pause, the baby in the basket will change all that. Because he is soon found in the river by the Pharaoh's daughter, who has come down to bathe with her women. Here she comes in her rich robes and her kohl-blackened eyelids, stepping into the water, moving toward the sound of the baby's cries, lifting him up out of his basket in delight, deciding in an instant to keep him, calling him Moses, which means lifted-from-the-water. And so the Hebrew baby is brought up at the royal court. And there he grows into a young prince, smooth-skinned, his eyelids now also black with kohl, sweet oils in his hair. But one day, as if struck by lightning, he will know something. He will know he is a Hebrew slave, and lead his people to freedom. And how does he know this? How? Will pauses. Goes on. He knows it the day he sees an Egyptian beating a Hebrew worker. "Faster," shouts the Egyptian, "work faster, you lazy dog." And seeing this, Moses suddenly realizes who he is. A Hebrew.

This is the best part of the story, this is the dream the story gives her. And Rainy spins away from Will's voice, from Moses, from the scene where he leaps and kills the Egyptian tormentor. She wheels and spins away from all the stories she has ever heard, running through her mind like the winter shadows on the snow, sliding slowly from west to east. And thinks only of the one story she needs, the one she longs for. To know. To know all of a sudden who she is, where she came from; to know what hands had placed her in the tree. To know if she had ever had a mother who nursed her. To know how she had come to Will and why.

Marie Bijou

"*Parlez français!*" says Marie Bé in a loud whisper to Pondy and Rose as they clamber up the steps into the train. "Speak French!" They enter the first-class compartment. With its carpets and cooler of iced water and plush velvet seats. They have paid, they have the right. "Speak French, it confuses *les américains*," whispers Marie Bé again. They sit down together, the three of them. Tightly together, side by side, heads high. Like a wall, like a fortress. Who shall dare question their presence here?

"I am not riding in the second class, I am not riding in the tobacco smell," she had said to Pondy. "I am not walking on spit and tobacco juice. We have paid, we have the right."

With a strident whistle and a great hissing of steam the train pulls out of the station. Rose feels as if she and her mother had no clothes on, naked, as if they had emerged from a bubble, their tiny kingdom now far behind them, the house in Serendipity surrounded by the mountain oaks where the world was defined day after day by the fortress of the trees and the sound of her mother's voice and the voices of Madame Gaby and her uncle

Jojo. She looks up from her seat between Marie Bijou and her father. Right across the aisle from them sits a pale girl with hair so blond it is almost white. She is holding a shiny brass cage on her lap. Inside the cage, two small yellow birds chirp and flutter. The white-haired girl notices Rose staring at her birds and gives her a hard look. She snatches up a blue silk cover from the seat beside her and slips it over the cage, sets the cage on the carpeted floor. Snuggling up to a stout woman next to her, she turns her back. Two long braids hang down, white against a dark blue velvet coat. Now the girl is whispering something to the woman, perhaps her mother. Rose hears the reply in a voice that the woman makes no effort to keep low. "They are just some frenchified niggers from New Orleans. Never you mind."

The train rumbles on. Early morning slowly moves toward noon. No one sits with them. Marie Bijou looks across the aisle. The white-haired child has the birdcage back on her lap. She has removed the cover and is clucking and whispering to her parakeets. Marie Bé turns her head away before the child can notice her stare. Outside, the train is passing a field of stumps. Logs to the market, she thinks. They must be on some flatboat by now, heading downriver to New Orleans. She pictures the river's huge muddy flow. Thinks of Pondy, before the war, working the river, day after day. A boatman even before Edouard Musson bought him in the Rotunda. A boatman from the cypress mills he had been, almost free, and carrying a gun. But with another name. The cypress people had called him Samuel. Until Simone Musson decided to change all that and call him Pondichéry just because she liked to hear the word. A name from faraway India. A name from her childhood home.

A long, melancholy whistle sounds from the locomotive. Marie Bé catches a glimpse of two young men sitting on a dirt pile. One black, one white. Maybe railroad workers. The black boy is passing a bottle to the white boy. They are laughing about something. And then they are gone from her sight. Now the train is rattling over a spindly bridge. Rose stirs in her sleep, her head is in her mother's lap, her feet on Pondy's knees. No. Pierre. Pierre. Marie Bé caresses her daughter's soft cheek. She glances quickly back at the girl with her birds. Their wings are flapping against the bars of the cage, making a soft yet urgent sound. She sees Gabrielle in a flash. Is it my fault, she wonders all over again. Did I push her too hard about the child, did I make her a prisoner in the shaded house? Or was there something more ominous, buried deep inside from earliest childhood. Did I push her to it to punish her, because I was brought up a servant and she was not? Did I hate her for this? Is my soul so dark?

"I am going now," she had said to Gabrielle. "I am not staying anymore here with you. Everything here is dying. You must not be so blind. Joseph will stay a little longer but not so much longer. His traveling time is coming. *Adieu, ma chérie.* I don't know if I shall see you again. I am going now."

Gabrielle had not turned from the window. "Go, go," she had said, her voice barely a whisper. "Go. It is better. Leave me. Be safe. Be safe with Pondy and Rose."

But as Marie Bé had crossed the threshold of the room, Gaby was suddenly behind her, touching her shoulder, and then they were holding each other tight. The feeling was unfamiliar and sweet.

"Be safe, *ma chérie*," whispered Gabrielle.

"*Adieu, ma* Gaby," answered Marie Bé. "*Adieu.*"

The conductor passes by, and since he has already seen their tickets, he just gives them a scowl with his mouth tightly closed in a thin line. When night comes, the burning cinders from the smokestack shower down around the windows and fly out into the dark.

Her mother she does not remember so well. And the pale, black-bearded man who came and went in the cottage on the rue de Rampart. Speaking to her *maman* in hushed tones, always kissing her hand when he arrived. Once she saw them early in the morning moving under the white sheets, the white lacy bedspread. And went quickly back to her room. Her *maman*. Octavie. The smell of amber. Her soft, deep voice. Her smile that felt like paradise. Edouard Monsieur Papa would always kiss the tops of their heads, hers and Jojo's. And always he would come with gifts. Building blocks, books, and dolls. And then all of a sudden they were both gone. Her *maman* and Edouard Monsieur Papa. And there was only Simone. Madame Simone Musson. And the two back rooms. And growing up with Gabrielle. Yet also a servant. Passing the plates to the guests, washing dishes, doing laundry. At least the music had not been lost to her.

But the music, this had begun before the time of Madame Simone. Because one day her black-bearded, white-faced papa had brought her a violin. "*Elle a de l'oreille,*" he had said to her *maman*. "*Tu l'enverras chez Valentin.*" Every Wednesday. And so she went, obediently, carrying the leather case containing the miraculous instrument. The learning had come easily to her. "Such a good ear, such excellent hands," said Monsieur Valentin, a mulatto with a high voice and odd lace cuffs quite out of style.

So even after she and Jojo had become servants in the house on Esplanade, the lessons had continued. But she no longer went to Monsieur Valentin. No, he came to them. Piano for Gabrielle, violin for Marie Bijou. First lesson at three o'clock for Gaby. Second lesson at four o'clock for Marie Bé. With the inevitable remark from Madame Simone each time she entered the parlor where the lessons took place: "Here is Marie Bijou Dumas, according to the last wishes of my husband." But soon there was just one long lesson for them both. She can hear Simone calling in her high-pitched voice, *"Monsieur Valentin est arrivé!"*

They played well together, she and Gabrielle. By the time Gaby was thirteen and she was fifteen they had mastered the pieces from Mozart for piano and violin. It was like being in a river together, flowing, whirling, rising, falling, rising again. At those times and at those times only, she knew they were truly sisters.

Simone

Simone Musson, standing like a tiny sentry on her wide front porch, is waiting, arms tightly crossed on her breast. Marie Bé is walking up the steps to her. Simone barely touches Marie Bé in greeting, whisking her quickly, quickly, into the house, then pushing at her back with her small hands, pushing her into the front parlor as if she were still a child, an old feeling that makes her sad. Marie Bé breathes in the familiar smell of turpentine and beeswax, and the faint scent of rosewater which always floats around Simone like a cloud.

She waits for the invitation to sit down. When it comes, it is more an order than an invitation. "And so? And so? *Alors?*" Simone urges. "Why is my daughter not here? Where is Gabrielle? Speak up, Marie Bé. And don't hide anything from me."

Marie Bé looks down at her hands, then straight up into Simone's dark and anxious eyes. She was beautiful once, Marie Bé remembers, though not so beautiful as Gabrielle. But now the lines of age are showing. The neck no longer so smooth, the little spots on her hands.

"Stop staring and speak up," snaps Simone. "I want the truth! If you lie even once I will know. I will know!"

Marie Bé stiffens and replies, "I am going to tell you now, and why would I lie? I am going to tell you how it was in this house behind the trees, this house of shadows and grief."

"Grief? What is this grief?"

Marie Bé takes a deep breath and begins.

"We were alone. It was the war. Monsieur Jared and Pondy, they were gone to the fighting. And our field hands, those of the farm, those who came with the farm, and who had no care for us, they soon were gone too, following the North Star. And so there was no more farm, no more fields. And then there was almost no more food in the town store. We must do something. We must do something. But what?

"So I find a farmer. I ask at the store and they tell me of this farmer, a man from the hills above the valley who has many fields up there. He came to help us. In the springtime. To plant a garden. It was this man."

Marie Bé fell silent.

Simone raised her voice. "Tell me what's what, Marie Bé. Go on. Don't leave anything out." Simone's face had turned pale; her eyes were now wide and frightened.

"It was this man from the mountain. Monsieur William Barnes. *Ma* Gaby she has feelings for him. She is grateful for his help. But there is more. She plays music for him. This man is in her heart. And one night he goes to her."

Simone crosses herself and bends forward as if in pain. She covers her face with her hands, elbows resting on her knees.

Marie Bé goes on.

"But after this, the man must return to his farm, to his wife and child. Because his wife, she has taken sick. And she dies. And the man, Monsieur William, he is so grieved he never comes back. I am certain he feels he has sinned, he feels he is punished by God, and so he is gone from us altogether.

"And then *ma* Gaby, after a time, she knows there is a child in her. But she will not have me take any message. Because Monsieur William, he gives her no sign. And so we hide everything. No one knows our secret. She stays in the house. I tell people she is ill. And I bring the child into the world, one night in February, with a full moon shining. A girl. We do well. It is a small baby, an easy birth for a first one."

"Why in God's name did you never tell me?" cried Simone. "How many times after the war did I come to you? How many times did you travel here? How many?"

"*Attendez*, listen to me, let me finish, listen. Soon we get a letter from Monsieur Jared, he is coming home. How can she greet Monsieur Jared with a child not his? How can she do this? And so we decide. I take the little one up the mountain, I leave her there, just close by in front of the house. There is a tree with a wide place where the trunk branches out. I choose this tree. I hide, I wait, I see Monsieur William and he takes her in. He knows. He takes her into his arms. And she is with him ever since. She is growing up with him and his son. She is well. She is loved."

Silence.

"Go on," says Simone. Her voice is almost inaudible.

"*Ma* Gaby, one day, she tells Monsieur Jared. She tells him all the secret, everything. And that is when he leaves us. But she cannot make herself go away from the place. She hopes and hopes. But there is no hope. I plead, I beg, yet I cannot make her leave. Now Joseph stays on to care for her, to stand guard over her. She must come home. This is true. And yet she will not do this. Impossible. She cannot do this. It is like a spell on her."

The talking is over. They both know it and they rise silently in a single movement and go to the door. There are no more words at all between them. Simone watches Marie Bijou through the wavery glass as she walks down the front steps, straight-backed, head high, down to the sidewalk and away. She keeps on standing there after Marie Bé has disappeared, staring out at the street, the trees, their white-washed trunks, their spreading leaves. Her knees feel weak, her head is slowly spinning. She grips at the door handle to recover her balance. Gabrielle, Gabrielle, she whispers. She hears again the sound of her husband's voice. "*Sois ferme*, Simone, be strict with the child. She will be a firefly, I can see it clearly, and she will make trouble if you are not firm with her."

But Edouard is long dead, long gone from her life. She is alone.

Sometimes she wishes her heart would freeze over, to ease the pain of those years after the war, the specter of poverty coming ever closer, and now this. She thinks about the new ice factory down by the river next to the railroad tracks on Tchoupitoulas Street with all the perpendicular pipes cooled from the inside by flowing ether while streams of water run down the outside. In two days there is ice, tons of ice, ice a foot thick. Enough to freeze her heart a thousand times over.

She imagines the mountain man, tall, lean, hands roughened by field work, face burned by the sun, a common man, and she pictures this common man with her daughter, Gabrielle Musson of the Mussons of New Orleans, her beautiful, small-boned, clever daughter with her wide-set dark eyes, her auburn hair, her delicate hands, her music. How could such a thing be?

Gabrielle

Gabrielle opens the big closet in her bedroom and reaches for the costume hanging there under a silken coverlet. She pulls it out and lifts the cover off quickly, throwing it over her shoulder and onto the bed. She shakes the costume a bit to make the sequins sparkle on the translucent pink and yellow wings. Where is the mask? Where are the gloves? Yes, there they are, up there on the shelf, all wrapped in tissue paper. She pulls down the light bundles, lays them on the bed as well, along with the costume. She undresses down to her petticoat. Now. First the satin gown of gray and brown. Soft, soft. Now the wings, still beautifully fitted over their wire structure. She slips them over her shoulders and fastens the hooks and eyes of the embroidered halter, thick with silver sequins. The fit is still perfect, keeping the diaphanous rosy wings precisely in place. She goes to the full-length mirror on the wall next to the door. The autumn dusk outside is briefly bringing a warm light into the room. She moves her shoulders back and forth, back and forth, giving movement to the wings, making them shimmer.

Now for the mask. She runs to the bed, pulls it from its nest of tissue paper, and lowers it over her head. Back to the mirror. Black eyes in a silver face, lustrous and black as coal with the little holes to see through and the silver surface still so shiny and the antennae bobbing with the pearls sewn to their tips. She nods and nods again to keep them moving. Now for the gloves. The long gray satin gloves. She pulls them on and they give off little puffs of dust. No matter. They are not ruined, they are fine. It is only the sequined slippers she cannot find. She stands barefoot in front of the mirror, turning to the left and to the right, swishing the skirt and nodding and making the wings sway back and forth.

Oh to be with Maman again, out on the upper balcony in the twilight, reclining on the long white cushioned couch, that good childhood time when their bodies rested easily against each other, and the pleasure of seeing out, able to watch the street without being seen, safe behind the ornate cast-iron railing.

She sways the dress again. Of course Maman always knew that Pondy was there, secretly following her and Marie Bé around at Mardi Gras. It was Maman who always had him come down from the plantation for the parade day. Gabrielle steps to the left, steps to the right, then turns as in a waltz. One two three, one two three. Her skirt flares out. Yes, she always had him come down so he could watch over us, so we would be safe. Maman liked to let us think that we had escaped on our own. That was her way. But she knew "for sure-sure," as Marie Bé would say years later. Marie Bé. She must have her bee costume somewhere back home. Maybe Pondy kept it for her. Now maybe she will wear it again come Mardi Gras. Or perhaps she will want something new. Perhaps she will go to the Choctaw at the market who does the good embroidery for something new.

Not here anymore. Marie Bé. Not here. How strange. Gone. Gabrielle feels hollow. The way she did when Marie Bé went away the first time, after Jared came back. Left her to her husband. *You will manage. Zadie from the store, she can come to clean and cook. You will be fine.* But she wasn't fine, no, not fine at all. And soon she had written to Marie Bé, begging her to come back, just for a little while, that she couldn't manage without her. But this was not true. It was only because to hold the secret was too hard for her alone. Too hard to live alone with the memory of Marie Bé's running feet, pounding down the stairs to the kitchen during that long, cold night, then climbing back up, bump, bump, bump, much slower, dragging the pail of hot water, then holding her belly on the sides, helping, coaxing. Talk to me, talk to me, she had cried. I can't do it without your voice. Make it come, make it come. And Marie Bé had chanted to her, molding her belly, "Big one, big one, yes, yes, a big one there, big one, big one, big one, sing in your head, *ma chérie*, sing with it, sing, sing, the child is coming soon. Soon, for sure-sure, soon, soon." And at last the tiny girl in her arms, all wrapped up and warm with the sweet baby smell against her cheeks. And the huge moon sailing high above the trees and so bright the winter fields had shone like day.

But it was too hard, above all, to live alone with the memory of what came afterwards.

Alma

The sun is sinking on the level plain. Jared Balfour and Alma Westerwald are walking out toward the still-fiery horizon, arm in arm, speaking companionably, at ease with one another. The westward-traveling coach has gone its way for many days now. Tonight there will be no travelers coming to the way station. He slips his arm around her waist, marveling at the sensation of joy that this simple gesture brings to him, and they walk on together, Alma adjusting her pace to his slight limp. They walk so far that, seen from the way station, they have become two tiny figures on the horizon.

As they slowly return, the stars have begun to show. She is telling him how she once went to the theater in St. Louis, to the opera, with her brother, way before they came out west, way before the solitude had become unbearable for him. And he had gone home and she had stayed. The music and the singing, so glorious. She has found this word, *glorious*. He watches her face in profile, her soft lips, the serious way she searches for her words, struggling to be as clear as possible.

He thinks that he would like to take her to the opera just to watch her reacting to the music and the singing and the bright stage. And then to talk with her about the performance. This would be good. To take her to the opera in New Orleans.

Later, seated in front of the fireplace, their hands joined, Jared feels his blood running like hers under their palms.

Alma moves her hand in his, leans toward him in the firelight.

He is back in the war. It is like a strange place he has not visited for many years. The words feel strange in his mouth because he has never spoken them before.

"We just lay there shooting without knowing what we were shooting at. You cannot imagine the sound. It was like we were all invisible, Yanks, Rebs, all invisible to each other there was so much smoke. It was like it was the forest itself that was the enemy. I pushed myself up on one elbow and I knew then that the two fellows on either side of me were dead. I didn't know what to do. I just began crawling forward on all fours. But it felt like I was blind. And the ground was uneven, like a stormy sea under my body. That was when I got hit. A shot to the hip. Felt like a tree had fallen on me. I couldn't move anymore. There were all these fires everywhere, on the ground and roaring in the treetops. And the ground fires, they kept coming closer to where I was lying. I yelled for help. If the fires had gotten to me, I was done for because of the packets of gunpowder in my belt. I must have passed out, because when I came to, Pondy was carrying me on his shoulder. God only knows how he found me. He got me to the Plank Road somehow and put me on a wagon and that's how I made it to the hospital tent. After they stitched me up they told me my hip was broken, there was nothing for me but to keep still. I was given six months' leave and we went home to North Carolina. And then the war was over."

He stops. For a time they listen to the hissing and crackling of the fire. He can't find a way to tell her about the hospital camp, the heap of amputated arms and legs, the smell. A pile of death as high as his waist.

Alma leaves him to his silence. But then she pushes him forward again.

"And so, when you came home?" she asks.

"After that, Pondy went back to New Orleans. He had been a boatman on the old Musson plantation, but he was a carpenter as well and he had work in a furniture shop. He took Marie Bé and Rose and Joseph back with him. But my wife pleaded and begged until Marie Bé came back with her brother and her child. To help out. Or so I thought.

"Something was wrong in my house. Something shrouded, hard to sense. But it was there, like a pall. It was the same house, same surrounding trees, same furniture, same unprofitable practice, same young wife. But with a shadow hanging over it all. It took me a long while to understand. She was good at hiding things, at covering up, at laughing and going on to something else, at always changing the subject when I felt she was about to tell me the truth. She was a shifting stream.

"I began to understand when she started going to her piano on some evenings. And mostly it was to play an old French song from her childhood. She would play it and sing it always just about sundown. You know, when it's no longer daytime but not yet night. It was the hour she always called *entre chien et loup*, the hour between dog and wolf. That's when she would go to the piano and sing that song."

"And what was this song?" asked Alma quietly.

"I remember this part." Jared recited the words in French. *"Chante, rossignol, chante, toi qui as le coeur gai, Tu as le coeur à rire, moi je l'ai à pleurer."*

"Tell me what is the meaning," said Alma.

"It means," answered Jared, " 'Sing, nightingale, sing on, you who have a happy heart, You have a heart for laughter, but mine is a heart for tears.' "

"And then?"

"And then always came the refrain, over and over at the end of every verse. *Il y a longtemps que je t'aime, jamais je ne t'oublierai.*"

Alma waited.

"And that means," said Jared, " 'I have loved you for so long, I shall never forget you.' "

The fire crackled on. They stay there, not moving, hands joined.

"All this," says Alma after a time, "is not your fault. Nor hers either."

Jared lifts Alma's hand to his lips. He kisses her palm and turns it and keeps it pressed against his cheek.

Robert Ray

Fever's got him. But he knows the cure. He has made the bitter drink of herbs and drunk it down. Sweating under the thick fur hides, his senses dulled, he can let his mind wander back to the old days. The days of the store. Yes. The days when he ran the village store. There were black-painted letters over the door. They spelled *Kincaid General Store*. Inside there was sugar, flour, salt, molasses, bacon. Calico. Salt pork. Dried beans. Twenty-five cents for this, a dollar fifty for that. The general store in their village above the moving river. Where you wade out and dip in seven times when the yellow leaves have fallen onto the water. For health. For a strong spirit. There were many cabins. There was their cabin. Dried clay between the logs. Their cooking pots. Their crops. Corn, beans, peas, squash, melon, pumpkins, potatoes. And the smell of the dust from the cornfields on their clothes. Yes. All this. Before the soldiers came. Not the Yankee soldiers. The other ones. The ones who came when he was young with her. Years. Yes. They had had a life of years. He and she. The front door painted blue. And the candle in the window every evening. To bring the whippoorwill close, she would say. She. Tayanita. So its song would give them sweet dreams. And so it went. On and on. Until the soldiers and their guns, until they were herded like animals into the stockade at gunpoint, until they were pushed onto the endless winter trail by the soldiers with their guns. Until the freezing death watch under the big rock, far from home. Until the three shallow graves in a wood on the side of the road. No marker, no nothing. For his wife and the two children. Tayanita. Ama. Salal. Until he lost his mind. And the boozing and the whoring and the wandering. And seeing the rivers so full of sand they were like a thick soup, the treacherous southwestern rivers where nothing could live, bearing huge masses of sand to the Mississippi and all the way down to the Gulf. And until the train. Yes. Until he drove the steam, years later, and year after year, his face black, his hands and arms black from shoveling the coal into the fire. Water tower to water tower, endless flat land, the melancholy whistle and the showers of sparks flying backwards all night long like fiery snow.

And so, when he finally returned to North Carolina, when he saw the Creole going up the mountain with her bundle, he guessed right away. He had caught the scent of what was happening like an animal catches the scent of its prey. He knew about loss and he smelled it coming in the Creole's quick steps. And so, when the child was old enough to understand, he began to tell her the old Cherokee tales. To fill the empty place he knew was inside her. He liked to tell her how all the valleys and the mountains were created by the beating of an eagle's wing. To watch her rapt face absorbing the wonders. And how, when

Powerful was making the plants and the animals, only cedar and pine, holly and laurel were able to stay awake the whole time. So after the seven days, when Powerful was done, he said to them, "To reward you for staying awake, you will not lose your hair in the winter." And that was why they stayed green all year round.

Robert Ray would also explain just how the bear-hunting story could be read in the sky. Because, he told her, when autumn comes and you look up at the stars forming the big dipper, the bowl is upside down and this is the bear upside down and dead, and the stars in the handle are the hunters and their dog. But when spring comes, you see the dipper is not upside down anymore, it is upright and this is the great bear come back to life and being chased again across the sky by the hunters and their little tracking dog. She believed for a while. And then she didn't believe. But always she wanted the stories. Just like the mother, the woman down in the village, living inside the shaded house, a house that seemed to be hiding, needed the words he sometimes whispered up to her in the nights.

The child's voice sounds from his memory. She was still very small. It was another one of those sitting-down-by-the-river summer days.

But the little girl kept asking the bad questions, the ones that hurt. She would say, "You were like an Indian once, weren't you, a long time ago? What happened to your wife? What happened to your children? How come you won't tell me? Tell me like when you tell stories."

He hears himself answering her. "It's the past. It's dead and gone."

"Tell me anyway," she says.

He finds a way. "I live with ghosts," he says. "They are always around me. You can't see them but they are here. If I stay real still some days, I can see her down by the river with the two little ones. I can hear their voices."

"Could I see them?"

"No, I don't think so. Not like you would see a tree, or a chair. I see them in my mind's eye. That's how I see them."

"Well, maybe I could feel them when they're around, like you feel the breeze."

"No, I don't think so."

And he would go on quickly to another story. The more fantastic the better.

"That's not true," she would say to him. "You're fooling."

"No, I'm not," he answers. "I really am the man in the moon. Didn't I ever tell you? I got bored up there sitting on the old moon day in and day out, so I just slid down on one of my moonbeams and I landed right here on the banks of the Green and I built me my moon house and here I stayed."

"You never," says the little girl.

But after that, he and she always called his cabin the moon house. And soon Ben and Will did it too.

His mind wanders again. The fever lets him. He is in a town with muddy streets. He can't remember its name. One of many towns, all alike. Not much more than a settlement. There is a railroad station, a hotel. There are shacks made of rough boards. The only women are whores. He watches an old Indian, a Lakota man, very drunk, sitting in the mud. The Indian has a box of matches. He is lighting them one by one, scratching the flame into life then watching it burn down until it nearly singes his fingers. The Indian throws the used match into the mud and lights another one. He has given away a fine buffalo pelt in exchange for this wonder. He goes through the whole box of matches, down to the very last one.

Robert Ray remembers turning away in despair from the Lakota and catching a glimpse of himself in a window, seeing his filthy, bearded face, a blanket around his shoulders, a nomad, a brother to the drunk. He knew then he had to go back to the moving water, or die.

Gabrielle

Winter is full upon the valley, but still Gabrielle stays on in the freezing house, keeping a fire going in her upstairs bedroom. The official papers have come through the mail. She knows now. A special delivery from Mountain View, as there is no more post office in Serendipity. The house has been sold to a Mr. Fremont of Raleigh, who will take possession in the spring.

Marie Bé is gone, long gone. With the red and yellow leaves swirling and falling, with the pigeons flying south in large goings, with Pondichéry having come at last for her and Rose. She sees him lifting their trunk into the wagon, and then handing up the violin in its case, so carefully, into Marie Bé's outstretched hands. She sees the three of them disappearing down the road for the long trip home to New Orleans.

And now Joseph has moved into the downstairs bedroom to stand guard over her, to stay close. As they know he must. The unspoken link between them has grown stronger in her need.

It is a night of whispering snow, big flakes falling thick

and fast and making drifts. Suddenly Gabrielle hears the plodding sound of horse's hooves, close to the house. Throwing on a shawl she creeps downstairs in her bare feet just in time to see a tall figure coming up the steps to the porch. She pulls open the door, breathless, just as the man is kicking the snow off his boots.

"William Barnes," she whispers. "William Barnes, is that you?"

A strong hand closes tightly around her wrist, twisting it around, and she feels smooth satin being pressed into her palm.

"Leave us be, Gabrielle," comes the man's low voice, the familiar country accent, his fingers pushing, pushing the purse down into her hand. She feels the hard shapes of the jewelry under the satin. "Go home to your people. Sell these jewels if you are in need, and go home."

"My God, Will, have you no more to say to me?"

"The child is well. She is happy. God willing, she will grow up to be a teacher. She does not know of you. And I do not wish to remember you. Go home."

Still she clings to his hand. "Will, please, may I not see her? Don't deny me, Will, I beg of you."

But he pulls his hand quickly from her grip and is gone into the driving snow.

Gabrielle stumbles back into the house, clutching the purse. She goes into the dining room and places the little bundle in front of her on the table, her two hands covering it like a tent. She sits there in a slump, not moving. But slowly her head goes down over her hands and she begins to cry. A moaning and then a sobbing that shakes her whole body.

Her sobs fade after a time, yet she cannot move; she feels as if her body has turned to stone. Suddenly she senses a presence behind her and turns in the chair. Joseph is standing in the doorway. The young man's stare is patient and grave.

"You should not be down here in the cold, Madame Gabrielle," he says.

"Oh, Joseph," she cries out, sounding to herself like a child. "I am so wretched. What am I going to do?"

Joseph does not reply right away. He just stands there observing her, allowing the silence to flow by.

"Go back to bed, Madame Gabrielle, before you freeze," comes the reply. His tone is firm, a man's voice. "You are in no state to have a conversation. We will talk tomorrow, *demain, quand il fera jour*, in the daylight."

Gabrielle can hear the ring of authority. Joseph is taking things into his own hands, he is giving her orders. She obeys, almost grateful. Holding the purse to her breast, she creeps back up the stairs and slides back under the thick winter quilts, hands still clasped around the satiny envelope so recently touched by Will. She curls up like a fetus. Exhaustion sweeps over her and she sleeps.

She awakens to full sunlight, and the sound of Joseph hammering at something out in the barn as usual. This busy sound gives her the energy to rise. Down in the kitchen a fire is going, and she makes coffee, eats a cold biscuit, and begins heating a kettle of water for a sponge bath.

She sits in the hot water and squeezes the sponge, and the water runs down her back, between her breasts. She closes her eyes, moves her feet against the rough bottom of the tub.

Sometimes, in the nights, summer nights mostly, she used to hear a whispering sound under her window, a faint scratching like someone slowly, slowly sanding wood. Half asleep, she would slide silently from the bed so as not to awaken Jared, and creep to the window. A raspy old man's voice would sound, whispering up from the shadows below. "He made her a cradle today. He rocks her and she sleeps well."

"Who are you?" she would breathe, but the voice from the shadows never answered.

Other times the voice said, "Today she walked by herself. She is strong and healthy."

Soon Gabrielle learned to hear the scratching sound from her deepest sleep. The messages kept on coming, although sometimes months apart.

"Today she ate by herself with a spoon."

"She pulls a little wagon with her dolls in it."

"She is learning to read. She is a quick learner."

A faint scuffling of footsteps would follow, and then there would be nothing but the night.

The tub water is getting cold. Gabrielle reaches for her towel and wraps it around her as she steps out onto the floor.

"I know it's not much yet," Jared had said of the house when he and Gabrielle arrived in the little North Carolina town. "But we'll have it all fixed up in no time." His tone had been sprightly, eager. Everything was fun. And soon Jared would be the most prominent lawyer in the county. Of course, of course. They could not fail.

But Jared's many clients did not appear. And nothing got fixed. The floors stayed the way they were. In the bedroom upstairs there were two places where you could see straight through into the parlor below. Gabrielle put her fine rugs over the holes. And she and Marie Bé had gone to work on the dusty, cluttered kitchen out back. Sometimes, that first summer, weak with exhaustion, unused to hard work from morning to night, she would sit down in the rocking chair in the upstairs bedroom, placing herself in the path of the breeze. And suddenly Jared was gone to the war, joining a regiment in Raleigh and taking Pondy with him. The three slaves who had chafed under Jared's haphazard orders had run off, and she and Marie Bé were alone with Rose and Joseph. Joseph, good as a carpenter, but no help at all in the fields. And the fields had quickly gone to seed and weed.

Simone had sent funds from time to time, but one day Gabrielle and Marie Bé saw that they were going to run out of food.

And that was how it all began. Gabrielle closed her eyes and covered her face with the towel, rubbing, making the darkness last.

Will

"Behold, a sower went forth to sow, and when he sowed, some seeds fell by the wayside, and the fowls came and devoured them up. Some fell upon stony places where they had not much earth, and forthwith they sprung up because they had no deepness of earth. And when the sun was up, they were scorched; and because they had no root, they withered away. And some fell among thorns; and the thorns sprung up and choked them. But others fell onto good ground, and brought forth fruit, some a hundred fold, some sixty fold, some thirty fold. Who hath ears to hear, let him hear."

Will lets the words he knows by heart enter his mind like a piece of music. But now the visiting preacher has begun to give his sermon. The young fellow goes on and on in a pedantic way explaining about the fertile ground. But without inspiration. Will follows his own thoughts. The man should use plain farmer's words, he thinks. Words that make sense to people who work the land. Like the words in the seed catalogues, or in the farmers' journals. Words that mean what they say. The "good ground" being the man who hears the word of God and understands it. Hears and understands.

As they drive home from the church, Rainy rests her head against Will's shoulder, listening to the *slap slap* of the reins over Bella's wide back and the *thud thuddery thud thud* of her hooves. The hymns from church go winding, winding through her head. She listens to Ben and Will talking about the possible wheat crop. And then about the bees. "Spring is late," Ben is saying. "My bees are barely stirring."

She dozes and awakens to hear Ben saying, "I remember a smell from when I was real little. It was a sweet smell, like candy almost." And Will is answering, "That would have been your mama drying the sassafras chips on the stove for her sassafras tea." And then they are talking about how maybe they will go digging for sassafras roots in January or February and make up a nice big stock of dry chips for sassafras tea and put them up in tightly closed tin boxes to keep the flavor in.

Rainy pulls the blanket up around her waist. Then up to her shoulders.

Ben

It was in the spring, Ben remembers, leaning against his father as they keep driving home, *thud thuddery thud thud.* And it was what happened that spring day that had gotten him the bees. Rainy was little and they had driven over past Mountain View to a wedding that had taken place in a large clearing under a giant elm. And all day long he could tell that his father was thinking back to his mama, because Ben knew that Will had married her under the spreading branches of that selfsame tree. Will had gotten all quiet during the ceremony and the preacher talk, and when it was over he had looked away from the girl in her white dress hanging on the arm of her young husband under the dappling shadows of the elm. And he had stayed quiet, lying on the blanket propped up on one elbow and gazing out into the distance at nothing in particular. It was right about sundown, and the people were gathering up their baskets and the blankets they had spread over the wild grasses. Rainy had fallen fast asleep on their blanket and Will had made no move to wake her or to leave. And that was when he had wandered off without Will's noticing. He couldn't help it. He had wandered away toward the edge of the woods, wandered through the fading light toward the dark of the woods. Because he thought he had seen it again. Something pale flickering between the trees a little deeper in. He would take one step forward and the flickering would disappear. But then it would begin again, a little further away, a little deeper in. A step, a step, another step, and he was in under the trees and dark coming on, but there it was again, the flit, flit, flicker, and now no path under his feet. Another step, another step. And then a heavy hand came down on his shoulder and his father's voice sounded from behind him, low, concerned, frightened even.

"Ben, what are you doing here?"

He remembers his tears and how they had turned into sobbing and his confession pushing its way out.

"It's her. It's my mama. She's out there. She's lost. She wants me to help her. She can't get out of the woods."

And then being swept up in his father's arms as if he were still little like Rainy, and being carried quickly back to the clearing where the child was still sleeping in the near dark. And listening to his father's quiet, comforting words.

"There's no such thing as ghosts, Ben."

And being rocked back and forth in his father's arms.

"Your mama loved you and her love is with you, inside you. It's not a ghost, it's part of you."

And suddenly, as Will rocked him, having the clear memory of a tin plate whistle his mama had given him to hang around his neck on a piece of string. And he was to sound the whistle, to blow into the thin, flat opening to make a shrill sound when he was playing outside so she would know he hadn't wandered off.

And how, slowly, his trembling had stopped. And how all this was the way the bees came to him. Because, just a few days later, Will had brought home the Langstroth hive from the general store in Mountain View. And a few days later they had found a swarm. And they had shaken the tree together and with a thrilling *whomp* the great humming mass of bees had fallen right down into the hive and they had carried it off as fast as they could, before, as Will said, the bee scouts could get back from looking for a new place. You have to outthink the bees, Will had said, laughing. You can't get a thing from bees without a few tricks. And they had carried the hive all the way to Rainy's apple tree and left it there to hum and prosper.

Rainy

Rainy has caught cold; she is sick in bed and Will is taking care of her like he always does. First he fires up the stove, then he puts a warm rock to her feet and covers her up with piles of blankets to make her sweat. And then he gives her a drink made of ginseng root and honey, hot and sweet, in the blue mug. And when she is well settled, he sits by her for a while on a stool and they talk.

Rainy can tell he is happy with the pictures she has tacked up on the walls to hide the chinking. She chose them herself from advertisements in the newspapers. And she has also written out in her best longhand one of his favorite Gospel sayings on a piece of cardboard and nailed it up over the front door. *And why take ye thought for raiment? Consider the lilies of the field, how they grow; they toil not, neither do they spin; and yet I say unto you, That even Solomon in all his glory was not arrayed like one of these.*

She had carefully drawn a lily in each corner of the cardboard rectangle and she had been proud of the result. Better maybe, she thought to herself, than the elegant swirling lilies on the silver medallion, long gone from them.

Will is telling her about the time he saw Halley's Comet when he was a boy. "I recall that you could see it for days on end just about dark. It had an enormous tail bending toward the north. And every night it appeared higher in the sky and further south."

And yet, as he talks on about the comet, she hears the dark river more clearly than ever behind Will's soft, slow voice. She longs to ask him for something that she cannot define. If he answered her, if he answered her truly, she thinks it would feel like seeing the comet. Or a shining star. *Tell me a true thing*, she longs to say. *Tell me a true thing about me. Tell me what you are hiding.*

Will talks on and on, soothing her. She feels his kindness flowing around her, but something else at the same time, something that leaves her frightened. Like a little animal who fears the plunging owl. Like what Will had showed her once in winter, the light traces in the snow of a predator's wingtips and the tracks of a leaping mouse.

Simone

Simone Musson paces up and down in the parlor of her house on Esplanade, twisting and twisting a little lace handkerchief between her fingers and making plan after plan to go fetch her daughter back from North Carolina. From door to window, from window to door. The sound of the blacksmith's hammer resounds from Molière's down on the corner of Broad Street. *Tank! Deling ding! Tank! Deling ding!*

Yes, it is now absolutely necessary. Enough is enough. It must be done. Already the talk has started: everyone knows that Jared has left her. And that there is some scandal about them. But if Marie Bijou wasn't able to make Gabrielle come home, she, Simone, is now the only person who can accomplish this feat. And Simone realizes with a sigh that she will have to resign herself to the bone-rattling journey in order to carry out the unpleasant mission. Ah, *Seigneur*, she had been able to run a plantation alone after Edouard died, but she had not been able to control her daughter. *Une vraie sauvage*, wild from her earliest childhood. Simone had always hoped that she would find a steady sort of husband. But no, *évidemment*, Gabrielle had fallen in love with that silly Jared Balfour, good-looking, she'd grant that, refined, well read, sophisticated, but lost in his irony, everything a joke, not a bone of sense in his body. Oh, she had sniffed him out right away. She had read him like a book. But Gaby was smitten, fascinated, hopelessly enchanted, lost in her passion. There was no stopping them. And how they had danced together, how they had laughed together. And of course how beautiful they had looked together. Jared Balfour. *Quelle catastrophe*. Penniless, last son of a fading New Orleans family. And off to be a lawyer in some godforsaken corner of North Carolina.

"Gaby, Gaby," she had warned. "You are quicksilver, both of you. You are fireflies. You are too much alike. It will come to no good. And he has no money at all."

What had come was their wedding. And then the war.

Simone drifts away from her troubled thoughts and remembers the big spider she used to watch on the wall of her bedroom in Pondichéry when she was still her father's child, her mother's child, during the long-ago days in India. The spider was large but harmless. It had a muscular walk, something like a dog, swinging its hairy body back and forth as it moved down the wall. She remembers the smell of the spicy lentils bubbling over the kitchen fire in the rue Vysial. And the soft winter breezes when it was less hot. The lovely blue skies of December and January, not yet the white stifling heat of April, May, and June. And the silent Tamil servants moving through the house on their bare feet. And the house itself, her childhood home in the tiny French colony, with its indoor courtyard and the four great red columns rising to the square balustraded corridor on the floor above, then rising again to the roof and the vast terrace overlooking the temple. With its hundreds of multicolored gods. Years later, in Louisiana, Edouard had brought home a new slave, a tall, strong man bought in the Rotunda along with a fine landscape painting. She had paid no attention to his given name and decided to call him Pondichéry. Since Edouard had made him a boatman between the plantation upriver and the harbor, from time to time she would be able to say his name. She would hear the sound of her voice calling his name. *Pondichéry, how is the work on the levees? How many pounds of rice, Pondichéry? How many barrels of sugar today?* It brought her childhood close again, her mother's soft lap, and the smell of the eucalyptus trees in the mountains where they went to flee the sweltering summer months. She knows that if she had not met Edouard in Paris the year they went home to France, she might still be in India, married to some functionary, living day in and day out with the relentless heat and the relentless rains. She knows something else as well. She knows that if she had not met Edouard, she might still have an innocent heart.

"Keep them close," Edouard had said. Over and over. "If I die you must keep them close until they are grown, until they can make their way. There is no one else who can do this. And make sure they speak correctly. None of the patois. *Ne discute pas. C'est comme ça.* This is how it must be. They are mine, as you know, from before your time."

Before your time. He always used that phrase. And when he died, she had complied, swallowed her pride and had the rooms built at the back of the house. One for Marie Bijou and the other for Joseph. She called them her young servants to her friends. Her dear young servants. But everyone knew. The rooms she now must rent to make ends meet. *Ah, la sale guerre*, the dirty war.

She wanders back into the story called "before your time." The story she knows all too well of Octavie Dumas, the slave he took with him to France, a woman who was his slave but also his mistress. In Paris, he took her everywhere with him. To the Café Français, to the Procope, to the homes of his friends, to the opera, where she dressed in her spectacular turbans, the beautiful Octavie. Even to the monastery at Saint-Benoît-sur-Loire to show her the calm but treacherous wandering waters of the great river there, and then over the fields to the abbey church just because he wanted her to see the wonder of a little stone sculpture outside on the tower porch, at the top of a column, a devil and an angel fighting for a human soul, each pulling at one arm, and how the devil's face was always in shadow, at any hour of the day. And how, returning with him to New Orleans, after all these kind attentions, she had sued for her freedom because she had walked on the free ground of France. And how he had watched her do this, and how she had won in the court. And how he had, deep down, as Simone knew all too well, enjoyed her winning and had admired her for it. And then, forward, forward, to the years of her cottage with its little garden, dark palm and pale banana leaves peeking up over the high picket fence, and its fruit trees, pomegranate, orange, and pear. And the smell of the night jasmine. And the children coming, first Marie Bijou and then Joseph. And later, later, after Simone's time had come—"your time," as he always said to her but never really meant—her time in the big house on Esplanade. Yes, it had come indeed, with their splendid marriage in the Saint Louis Cathedral and the birth of Gabrielle, but it had never been truly her time because part of him was always gone, was always in the house and in the little garden on the rue de Rampart, near the orange trees and the pomegranate and the night jasmine. And then Octavie had died of yellow fever during a bad epidemic, he following quickly from the same disease. Even when they both were gravely ill, he had not been able to stay away from her. Because he could never stay away from her. Not for long.

Will

Will is dreaming. He is lost on an unfamiliar road. He is wearing old shoes too large for his feet. They have no shoelaces. He is dirt poor, his farm is lost, he scuffs along, not knowing where he is going, a vagabond, filthy and despised. He awakens in fear. And then he hears with unspeakable relief the dry whisper of the ticking inside the pillow under his cheek.

Quickly he turns his mind to work. They have begun to build a furnace, he and Ben. Yesterday they got in the anvil block. Today they will start on the shop doors. Oh, but her hands had been so cold and her voice so frightened. Why does she stay on, wretched woman? Why can't she leave him alone? Go away at last, back to her people. Be gone. Be gone. He realizes his fists are clenched in the darkness. The sound of the rain no longer makes him happy, nor the sight of the trembling grass, nor the soughing of the pines, nor the feel of the plow. Above all, the words for his journal no longer come to him. The precious ones that try to capture the flying clouds or the sound of the wind in the trees. He takes comfort in the knowledge that the children are sleeping. Warm under their thick quilts. Rainy in her cot behind the stove. Ben in his chosen private place up under the eaves. Will peers at his pocket watch hanging from a nail on the wall. It is one in the morning. Three hours more before time to rise. He turns onto his back and closes his eyes. But then she comes to him and he sees the turn of her head, her quick steps, her fluid movements when she danced around the room, that odd parlor room, half rich, half poor. And how he had watched her small fingers drifting over the keys like a mist, drifting and then sounding the notes so precisely and yet still so lightly. The music had pleased him, had brought him a feeling like seeing Arcturus just before dawn at the end of winter, yellow Arcturus, the star announcing spring.

The Creole had walked up to his farm one cold March evening, stepped right up to the door, knocking loudly. Ella had opened up, staring, astonished, at the tall brown woman.

"Will!" she had cried. "Come out here!"

"Monsieur William Barnes?" the woman had said in her strange accent when Will appeared. She stood at the foot of the steps, straight-backed, arms folded over her chest. "You are Monsieur William Barnes?"

"I am," Will had answered.

The woman did not waste words. "I come for Madame Jared Balfour. Who is name Gabrielle. We need help or we will go hungry. We have no one left, only me and my brother and one tiny girl child, my own. And *le maître*, he is gone to the war. And my husband with him. I hear in the town store you can perhaps help. A garden for food. We are of the city, we are of *La Nouvelle-Orléans*, we have no knowledge of these things. *Je vous en prie*, please, we have almost no more food. To plant a garden. We will pay. We can pay. You can come some days to help?"

The cold wind was blowing hard, but they did not ask her in. Then Will spoke. "What is your name?"

"I am Marie Bijou Dumas. I am free woman from my mother, *une personne libre de couleur*, free since before the war. But I stay here with my Gabrielle, for we are children together."

Ella had quickly slipped her arm into his as he answered. "You tell your mistress I will consider her offer."

"*Bien*, I will tell her," said the Creole. "You will know our house, the last in the village, with many trees around it."

And without another word she had walked swiftly away.

The March weather had turned warm the next day and the woods had begun to show a little green as Will drove the wagon down the mountain to the small valley town. He recognized the house at once. It seemed to be hiding behind a curtain of trees. Perhaps they had been watching for him, because they came out right away. The tall Creole with a baby on her hip and a boy whose resemblance to the Creole was striking. The brother, of course. A slim white girl, looking no more than eighteen years of age, stood in front of them in a dark red dress with elegantly pleated sleeves. She had large brown eyes, and her small hands were loosely clasped in front of her. Graceful, was his first thought. And then, with a twist of scorn, dainty. Dainty and spoiled, naturally. No help to anyone. Pretty, without a thought in her head, he wagered. Her auburn hair was thick, unruly, slightly tamed by a bun from which curls seemed to escape in every direction.

He bowed awkwardly to the little group as a whole, not

sure what the proper greeting would be. He was unused to seeing black and white people together, looking for all the world like a family.

Will straightened up and cleared his throat.

"Mrs. Balfour, how do you do. I am William Barnes. I have come to say that I will accept your offer. I will help you folks to plant a garden to see you through. But I want no payment for my help."

"We are very grateful to you, Mr. Barnes." The young woman had a low voice that took Will by surprise. Musical and warm. With more than a trace of the accent he had already heard in the Creole woman's speech. "I thank you with all my heart. This is a blessing."

She gave him her hand and he took it, holding it a moment longer than necessary because her grip was firm, surprising him again. And then their fingers slid apart and he was back on his horse and riding home, but he could still feel the touch of her small hand.

Will turns in the bed. Sleep will not come. He gets up and lights a fire in the stove for coffee. His old sin lies heavy on his heart. And heavier still the punishment that had come so quickly.

Rainy

Rainy has a mirror. It is a round hand mirror with a sculpted
wooden frame and handle, and it had once belonged to Will's
mother, who died when he was young. Rainy holds it to her face.
She knows she is pretty. She had known it for the first time in
the look of the horseman who had been so startled by her in
the woods. But would this beauty be a good thing? Will had
taught her that it was wrong to "call attention to yourself." This
was vanity. Better to learn to look out at the world, he always
said. To see, for instance, that shadows are blue. Look how that
red barn throws a blue shadow, he had said once, pointing. He
had taught her to learn the seasons, and the stars that announce
their coming and going. And how fog carries sound. And to
listen for the foxes barking in March.

But if you were beautiful, she reasoned, you couldn't help it
if people looked at you. She knows she likes to look into Robert
Ray's sad eyes; they are beautiful to her. She is drawn to them,
she always wants to look into those eyes. Maybe because she can
see her own sadness there. So does beauty have something to do

with pain? With hurting inside? Does it have to do with some-thing missing and longed for? And seemingly forever out of reach? Like the hunters in Robert Ray's story, the hunters going after bear who end up in the sky among the stars. Sometimes she wishes she were a star, twinkling up there in the cold. On days when they call her Rainy-No-Mama at school, or when they push her out of their jump-rope games and sing out, "Bird girl, bird girl, found in a tree."

A few days later, she is back up at the springs. It is a cold and cloudy day and no one is there. She walks between the rusting tables, running her fingers over their rough surfaces, peering into the windows of the old house, just the touch of her hands flaking the paint on the windowsills. She feels like she is not real, her arms hurt, her heart is heavy as a stone inside her. Heavy with the sad, the thing she cannot define that she calls the sad. She turns away from the crumbling house and walks up to the headwaters, listens to the rushing of the Green where it gushes up icy cold out of the mountain. She kneels down and puts her hand into the stream. She can feel the cold all the way to her bones. She tries to hear the breathing of the world, the way Will does when he gets real still. She is not sure that she can hear anything at all. But then, suddenly, like Moses in the story, she knows something. But it's not about what she is. It is about what she is not. No, she is not at all like those children who come to play around the old house up here by the springs. They are not her kind. She does not wear white lace dresses, she does not own black patent-leather shoes, she has never played with a porcelain-faced doll or had bouncing corkscrew curls that must be patiently created with a hot curling iron. She hoes, she plants, she sews, she mends, she chases wild pigs with a long stick, she reads books in the evenings, she hunts for scuppernongs down by the river and eats them, spitting out the bitter skin and seeds. She gathers strawberries, she picks the beans and the tomatoes, she digs up potatoes, she makes biscuits and corn bread, she goes to school when she can but she knows many things you don't learn in school, yes, and she is proud that she knows that a red barn casts a blue shadow, and how fog carries sound, and how to read the seasons in the stars. And yet, and yet, she knows that the answer has got to be down there, it's got to be down there somewhere among those people. The place where Papa Will never goes, the place he avoids like the plague, the place he never wants to talk about. It's got to be down there, the answer to where she came from. Down in Serendipity.

She must be like the hunters in Robert Ray's story. And she knows what she has to do.

Joseph

Serendipity is almost a ghost town, a ghost town except for them. In the empty houses dust gathers in the parlors, on mirrors and mantelpieces, it penetrates the upholstery of abandoned armchairs left uncovered, thickens on battered pots and pans in the kitchens where no fire burns. The men and women who lived there have disappeared, gone to other lives. And the chanting children, all gone too. In their house behind the trees, Joseph sleeps downstairs now, where Marie Bé and Rose used to sleep. He knows this to be his responsibility, to watch over her. He has been in and out of some of the empty houses, raiding, picking up a few jars of preserves here, an extra blanket there.

He sees Gabrielle walking out into the pale spring sunshine. He beckons to her from the shadows of the barn. "Madame Gabrielle," he calls in his man's voice, more distinct and a little louder now that he is her guardian. "Madame Gabrielle, I want to show you something. *Venez*! Come!"

She enters the barn. The morning sun is streaming in,

lighting the far wall. Joseph comes forward, holding something in his hand. She looks down and sees lying on his open palm the whitened skeleton of a small bird. He lets her stare at it. Then he speaks up.

"You see this, Madame Gaby," he says quietly, "look well, look close. Look close before it is too late. You must take your foot out of the grave, madame. You don't even know you got your one foot in, *n'est-ce pas?* *Un pied dans la tombe.* You don't even know that, do you?"

He lifts her hand gently and tips the skeleton into her palm. It has no weight at all. He whispers, "Do you wish to be a ghost? Do you want your soul to become like these little bones? If you close your fist, you will crush them."

She sees Will then, in a rush, smiling at her, and she hears him saying, "We walk by faith and not by sight." Will. Who wants her gone. Who wants her gone.

On the far wall of the barn, there is a long, wide shelf where Joseph has stored dozens of objects, the fruits of his scavenging expeditions into the abandoned houses. She approaches the long shelf and its objects all lit up by the morning sun. There are useful things like pots and pans and jars of preserves, but there are also porcelain-faced dolls, their stuffed bodies smelling of mildew, old pewter pitchers, dusty glass bottles, croquet balls that have lost their colors, and a mallet split with age.

Joseph stands behind her. "Look, Madame Gaby. Look well. What are these? All dead things from dead houses. All broken things, all throwaway things. Is this what you want to be, a throwaway thing? You must have the courageous soul, Madame."

She stands there for a time looking at the shelves. She doesn't notice that Joseph has disappeared. Finally she places the feather-light skeleton next to an oyster shell.

She closes her eyes. She allows herself to remember Will, she lets the feeling come. She lets it take its full course. How she had left her door ajar that one time, that one summer evening when he had worked late on the garden and she knew he had not gone home. And how she had placed a little candle burning in its pewter holder in the doorway on the floor. And hearing his quiet steps on the stairs at last in the dead of night. And the candle rising in his hand when he came into her room, and how, before turning toward her, he had set it on the chest of drawers next to the little silver horse, and how the flame had glimmered on its flanks and mane and tail.

Gabrielle walks back into her silent house. She tugs on the top drawer of the big buffet, pulls it open and takes out the old cleaning cloth, spreading it wide on the dining room table. Now she begins lifting out all her silver. Out of all the drawers, one deep drawer after another, all the silver from her mother. The heavy forks and knives, the soup spoons, the dessert spoons, the serving spoons, the long-handled ladles, the little hollow *coupelles* for salt and pepper. And then, from the glass cabinet, the fat teapot, the big round trays with their knobby edges, so hard to clean properly, the coffee service. Mindlessly, she applies the silver polish to all, rubbing the creamy substance in with an old rag until her fingers are black. Then out back to the kitchen where she pours boiling water over each batch. And back to the big table again, where she polishes each piece with a clean cloth. On and on she works. By late afternoon, she has finished. Joseph still seems to have disappeared; they have made no dinner. She bends forward, lays her head on her arms, and falls asleep right there in the acrid smell of the silver polish.

Rainy

It is the middle of the night and there is only one light that she can see in all the town. It is faint, coming from a house that seems to be hiding behind a circle of trees. She walks along the unfamiliar road, careful not to stumble in the dark, moving closer and closer to the trees and the flickering light shining through. As she approaches, she can see that the light is coming from a window to the left of the front door. She moves forward along the path leading to the house, passes under the trees and walks up the front steps, crosses the wide porch to the door. She turns the handle and pushes it slowly, quietly.

The door is not locked; it opens easily. And then she is inside the silent house. From the entrance hall she looks to the left, through an open door, toward the light. It comes from a kerosene lamp flickering in the middle of a long table. A woman is seated there, bent forward, her head resting on one arm. She seems to be fast asleep. The table is covered with polished silverware, gleaming in the flickering flame. The woman sighs, but does not come out of her sleep. Rainy crosses the threshold and enters the room. Slowly she walks around the table, smelling the house, listening to the woman's quiet breathing. She looks at the woman, her head resting sideways on one arm, her thick, curly hair coming out of its bun, her cheeks and fingertips smudged with stains from the silver polish.

Rainy does not know how long she stands there, looking at the lady. Finally she backs out of the room and goes silently out of the house. She makes the long walk back, up through the leafy forest, then up through the pines, over the log bridge, over the rushing river water, past Robert Ray's darkened moon house, then more forest path all the way to the wheat field and then home. Removing only her shoes, she slips into her bed behind the stove.

The house is silent. The honey from Ben's bees sits in tightly covered glass jars on the long shelf next to the strongbox. On the big table where Will left them lie the April issue of *The Planter* and a seed catalogue. Some night sounds from the forest reach her ears. The hoot of an owl. The faint bark of a fox. In Will's fields, the grains of wheat and corn have begun their slow swelling, and in his vegetable garden, underground and unseen, the seeds of beans and cucumbers are sprouting into the earth. Near the front door, its white blossoms like stars in the night, the apple tree is in bloom again.

Gabrielle

Gabrielle sleeps on. She is dreaming she is with Marie Bijou and they are standing in front of the house with the trees at their back. And she sees again the ladies of Serendipity, the ladies of the little town. They are walking toward her and Marie Bijou as if in a parade. Not like a Mardi Gras parade with music playing and everyone in costume, and people on the big floats disguised as fantastic birds and beasts, with diaphanous wings or animal heads bobbing and the crowds running along on both sides. No, this is a parade of ghosts. Here they come, here they come, now they are passing right in front of her, but too close, too close in their swishing silks. She lifts her hands to push the women away with their suffocating perfumes, their mincing steps, their hard eyes. "Get away from me!" she cries out in her dream, pushing, pushing to keep them at arm's length. And she hears Marie Bé hissing at them from behind her. There they go, chattering and giggling and staring back at her. And one of them is whispering to another, "Look, it's that New Orleans hussy, New Orleans hussy, with her nigger, with her nigger." And she awakens from her nightmare.

It is still full dark. She goes to the door and pulls her shawl from the knob, using it to wipe the smudges from her fingers. She throws it over her shoulders and walks out into the night, down the village road, then taking the path leading up into the foothills. She walks faster as the path leads up under the trees. The forest is very still. As the sky grays, a small breeze begins to blow, bringing the sharp sweet smell of the pines. Birds have begun to call out. Her legs feel stronger now. Although she does not increase her pace, she knows that there will be no turning back. It was on just such a long night that Marie Bé had gone on her mission, thinking to save her from shame. On just such a gray morning before sunup that Marie Bé had laid the baby in the cleft of the apple tree. Hadn't she heard it a thousand times and yet begged to hear it again and again. "Yes, *ma* Gaby, I laid her there and I hid and watched. And by and by, I saw Monsieur William come out of the house and walk down to the tree and he picked her up and carried her right back in. He held her close like he knew who she was, like he knew she was his own child."

She had left the light on the floor at the door to her room, left the door ajar. And called to him wordlessly. And when he had come to her at last, when he had knelt down on the floor beside her, he had only said, "I want to hear you say my name." And she had answered, "William Barnes."

Now she has reached the clearing. As she walks toward the house, the door opens and there is Will.

They do not speak.

He comes down the steps and stands before her. He takes

her hands into his hands. They are the same hands as then. Slowly she leans forward until her head is resting on his breast.

"It is all right to love, William Barnes," she whispers. "It is not forbidden."

Slowly, slowly, she feels his arms as they go around her and pull her close.

Robert Ray

Down by the river, Robert Ray is having his springtime dream again. He is following the Cherokee hunters. He can see them just ahead of him, through the trees, running easily. He tries to catch up, but they remain ahead of him, loping along effortlessly. He can hear the barking of the little tracking dog. Suddenly they begin to rise, and now they are running on the air, yes, he can see them, there they go, running up and up on the air, rising past the dark branches of the pines. But then Robert Ray feels the lift under his own feet as well. Now he is with them, right behind them, and the forest, the river, the big mountain, all lie far below. They are all running up and up into the night sky, they are passing the shining star creatures. He is with the hunters and soon they will catch the bear. He is one of them and they run on together.

Pierre Lebois

In a photographer's studio in New Orleans, three French windows stand open to the street, letting in the warm spring air and the springtime sounds. Facing these high windows, Marie Bé, Pondy, and Rose are seated on a sofa upholstered in green velvet. Behind them hangs a canvas backdrop painted in blues and greens and pinks representing an island in the Mississippi River complete with palm trees and giant orchids and flamingoes. Stiffly sitting, they know they must not move. The moment is crucial because the photographer has now hidden his head and shoulders under the black cloth. "*Attention!*" he calls from under the cloth. His hand slips forward, he is opening the lens, removing the cap to let the light stream in, the light that will transform itself magically into an exact image of the three of them on the thin metal plate deep inside the camera. They keep as still as statues. They listen to the grandfather clock standing up against the wall to their right, as its heavy pendulum behind the glass door swings back and forth, sounding its slow and regular beat. This will be the first of their coming-home pictures. Both will be placed on the mantelpiece in frames. Commemorating the time they were home at last after the long separation. For the second picture, the photographer asks them to stand and step forward. He pulls down a plain white background from a roller on the ceiling. *Tick-tock, tick-tock*, goes the clock. Pondy, Pierre Lebois now, holds himself tall between his wife and daughter, a hand on each of their shoulders. As he stands and waits, Pierre is recalling the day he first laid eyes on Marie Bijou.

Among his name times, it was during the years when he was no longer called Sam, after his cypress lumber master died, and he had found himself in the Rotunda in New Orleans on a block. And being purchased by a black-bearded, pale-faced Frenchman who took him away along with a large painting. But it was years before he saw her. And that day was a day of clouds flying, a day of joy even if he was still a boatman, still a slave, with the calluses from pushing the pole on his hands and on his shoulder, no longer moving the cypress lumber but a load of rice and sugar down to the harbor. And known by a new name from the Musson mistress who had wanted to hear this name spoken, this strange-sounding name of Pondichéry, a sound that was sweet to her ears. Had wanted to hear this name from the first time she saw him, when her pale-faced, black-bearded husband was still alive.

Yes, it was his Pondichéry name time when he first saw Marie Bijou. She was standing a few steps apart from the white family, apart from the straight-backed Musson mistress and her little daughter. Turning her back on the tiny straight-backed Musson mistress, now a widow. Yes, there she was, standing apart, a very young girl, no more than sixteen, looking out over the water, but his love was born in that instant seeing the bright eyes, the long limbs, a red headscarf that could not hold down all the wild hair blowing back and forth. Harbor wind, river wind blowing, and his soul like a bird. Because, after seeing her, there was never another for his heart. And when she extended her hand, all shy and confused, yet calling him *monsieur*, as if he were a free man, saying, "Bonjour, Monsieur Pondichéry," he had known he would wait as long as it took for her to be ready.

Marie Bijou

Joseph is leaning out the second-floor window of the shop on Chartres Street, right over the sign that says "Pierre Lebois, *menuisier.*" He is holding a long-legged puppet from its strings, a Pierrot puppet in a white clown suit with its three black buttons and a ruffled collar. He is swinging it back and forth to attract the attention of passersby. "Step right up," he sings, jiggling the puppet's wooden head and hands and feet, making it dance and sway and knock against the wall. "Step right up, *messieurs, mesdames*! Come in, ladies and gentlemen, come in and have a look. There is something for everyone in this shop. Hand-painted bowls! Wooden ladles and spoons! Rocking chairs! Our chests of drawers are the very best, *ce qui se fait de mieux*! See our beautiful *semainiers*! Seven drawers, one for each day of the week!"

Standing in the doorway below, Marie Bijou listens to her brother calling to the people. A vendor is approaching, a woman calling out, "Beautiful callas! Buy my callas! Hot hot! *Tout chauds*! And Marie Bijou sings out as well from her doorway, adding her voice to the music of voices: "Fine tables! Fine chairs! Fine tables! Fine chairs!"

She hears her husband, her Pierre, inside, laughing with a customer. Soon Rose will join them, coming to help out at the shop after school.

They are home. The crape myrtle is there, in full springtime bloom, with its smooth polished trunk, pushing up out of the brick sidewalk. The high picket fence, the creaking wooden gate she would swing back and forth on when she was little. And the big central room with its stout table and chairs that seem like old and faithful friends. And the garden, dark palm, pale banana, the fruit trees, the night jasmine, everything from before. Their mother's cottage. They will have the pink blossoms of the crape myrtle all summer long, they will watch its leaves turn red and orange in the fall. Suddenly she sees her mother, hears her soft, low voice telling the story for the hundredth time. "I walked up from the big river with your papa when we were in France and he led me across the fields to the old abbey church and there he shows me the sculpture, at the top of a column, the devil with the shadow on his face from morning to night. No sunlight ever touches his devil's face, while he tugs and tugs at a poor soul, a man, to try to take him down to hell. But there is an angel on the other side and he is tugging too. And the angel will win out, I can see this. Just like me. Just like I won out when I was standing in the courtroom after we came home, and I could see in the eyes of the judge before he opened his mouth that my plea would be answered, that I spoke the truth and that I was free because I had walked on the free ground of France. And the next day, the very next morning, I walk out before sunrise and I go to the *pointe* so the first rays will fall on my free face."

Joseph goes on dancing the puppet.

Other street voices well up like a river flowing by the shop.

Pralines! Pralines! For your sweet tootheeeee!

Hominy man!

Come out today

Buy my sweet hominy!

Scissors! Scissors!

Grind 'em sharp

Mighty sharp

Sharp a cut a gullet out!

Horseradish! Horseradish!

Cantaloupes! Cantaloupes!

Smell 'em! Smell 'em!

Rags! Rags!

Old bottles!

Brass and copper!

Clothes! Clothes!

Sand! Want sand!

Sand your doorsteps

Sand your floors

Want saaaandeeeee!

Jared

Upstream, between Baton Rouge and New Orleans, the great Mississippi is over a mile wide. There is some early morning fog, and the air is also filled with smoke from the burning of the sugar cane stalks on the plantations that line the banks. A steamboat is making its way downriver, keeping to the safe deep water in the middle where the current is strong. Two travelers on their way to New Orleans, a man and a woman, are leaning on the railing of the riverboat's passenger deck, marveling at the feeling of being on a shoreless sea. Suddenly they hear men's voices singing, but they cannot see through the misty, smoky air. "Dance de boatmen dance," go the voices, "oh dance de boatmen dance. Dance all night till broad daylight and go home wid de gals in de mornin'." The couple are straining to see where the singing could be coming from when the silhouette of a flatboat emerges right under them, perilously close to the towering flanks of the rumbling steamer, and they hear frightened shouts, cursing, catch a glimpse of a swinging lantern and the shadows of men running along the deck of a small wooden craft. But their huge craft passes swiftly, leaving the flatboat rocking in its giant wake. After a time the air clears up and the man and the woman turn away from the railing and walk slowly along the deck, returning to their stateroom. The man has a slight limp, the woman, sturdy and blond, hangs on his arm, her head inclined toward his, a long braid hanging down her back.

Rainy

The light is fading; darkness has begun to fall. They are together, the three of them, on the front porch of the farmhouse. Rainy is sitting on the top step. Will is on the porch seat. The woman is beside him. And Rainy knows her as the sleeping woman from the valley house. That her name is Gabrielle. She and Will are sitting close together. Her arm is under his arm, their hands are joined. They have been walking in the forest all day long. Rainy has her back to them, but she can feel their arms, their hands. Entwined. Touching. She doesn't know what to do with this feeling. Where is Ben? Has he run off somewhere for a while? No. He is with Robert Ray. Learning how to make a lure. Or maybe setting some traps. She listens to the crickets. After a while, the sound seems to be turning into waves of energy; she can almost see them eddying up out of the dark. A mockingbird calls from the woods. A big moon is coming up over the pines.

Still, Rainy lets the moments slip by. Everything is strange and yet peaceful. She watches the moon. Long enough to see it move a little higher.

"Tell me," Rainy says at last in a whisper, still not looking at them. "Tell me. Tell me."

Will's voice is low but clear. "Rainy, we are here together because I am your father. Your real father. And this is your mother."

Rainy turns toward them, and as she turns, the woman rises and steps forward quickly, lightly, and sits down beside her on the top step.

"You see that moon?" she says, and, as she speaks, Rainy feels the woman's arm slip gently around her shoulder. "The night you were born, there was a moon just like that. It was so bright, the fields shone like day." The woman's arm has begun to tremble, but around her shoulders it stays. Rainy turns and looks into the woman's eyes. They are dark and soft. Like hers.

And then she feels Will's tallness behind her. He sits down on the other side of her, his arm reaches around her, and she is held in her parents' embrace.

Epilogue

SUMMER

Will is driving the wagon up the path to the farm. He urges the mare forward, but carefully, keeping her at a slow, steady pace. Behind him, protected by blankets and firmly roped to the sides of the wagon, is Gabrielle's upright piano.

Rainy and her mother are walking together on the other side of the wheat field. They are walking slowly, arm in arm, leaning in toward each other. Will doesn't need to know what they are saying. The sight of them is enough.

Ben comes running to help him unload the piano. Together they undo the ropes, pull back the blankets, and slide the piano slowly off the wagon, balancing it on a board Will has pulled down from the back of the wagon, making a chute between the wagon and the ground. Using the same board, they push the piano up the front steps. Slipping one of the blankets under its feet, they push the instrument into the house.

AUTUMN

From the farmhouse comes the sound of a piano, of someone playing scales. Inside, Gabrielle is speaking to her daughter. "Your hands, *ma chérie*, they must be just over the keys, fingers slightly bent ... yes ... just like that. Good. Now we begin again."

Down by the river, near the log bridge, Ben and Robert Ray have returned from setting beaver traps further downstream. They have finished their work. Now Robert Ray is pulling off his shirt and overalls. He wades into the river because, as he says, this should be done now, in the season when the yellow leaves fall onto its surface. He dips in seven times, immersing himself. "For your health and your spirit," he says to Ben. Now Ben is pulling off his own shirt and overalls. He wades in too, imitating the actions of the old man as precisely as he can.

WINTER

Down in New Orleans, Simone Musson is beginning to feel her age. Her joints ache when she gets out of bed in the morning. And life is not easy. She still must take in boarders. She still must skimp and save. But she has peace now. In the spring she will travel again to the farm in North Carolina. She knows the man is a good man. His ways are foreign to her, but she sees the love. And the girl, the girl they have decided to call Simone but who still has the name like rain, she is a wonder. And soon she, the elder Simone, will bring her for a long stay in New Orleans. Her granddaughter.

Jared and Alma Balfour have moved into their new three-story house. It stands on one of the steep hills in San Francisco, looking out over the harbor. A metal plaque is visible from the street: *Jared Balfour Attorney at Law*. He has so many clients these days he must turn some away. Alma is pleased for her husband. For them both. For herself. But from time to time, she misses her old life. And when those moments take hold, she likes to tell Jared how she came to love the treeless prairie and how she learned to hear its voices, the different birdcalls and, above all, the wind which has a sound like a great outrushing breath when it moves through the grasses. And how the moving grasses let you see the wind. One day she will also tell these things to their little son.

SPRING

Will writes in his journal. "Wind so strong today it blew my old hat right off my head and it went sailing over the trees. For all I know it may be flying still. Reading Seneca's 'Morals.' Rainy came running in from the garden this afternoon with something cupped in her hands. She opened them like a book and there lay three ripe strawberries, the first of the season." He has begun to find the words; they have been coming to him the way they used to do. Some came today for the early morning light. Maybe this will happen again. Soon, he hopes.

A framed photograph of Octavie Dumas, an old daguerreotype, sits on the mantelpiece in the cottage on the rue du Rampart with the other family photographs. She is formally dressed with an elegant turban artfully wound and tied around her head. Some evenings, after a long day at the shop, Marie Bé takes a moment to look at her mother, and when she does, if there is silence in the house and a feeling of peace, it seems to her that the smell of amber is all around her and she loses herself for a few moments in the woman's gaze.

A List of Things

One solid silver bracelet, jade inlay.

One copy of *Pilgrim's Progress* with field flowers pressed inside the pages. Owner signature on flyleaf: *William Barnes.*

One chest of drawers, known as a *semainier,* with seven drawers, one for each day of the week, oak, hand-carved, signed *Joseph Dumas, Menuiserie Pierre Lebois, New Orleans.*

One copy of "The Hive and the Honey-Bee" by the Rev. L. L. Langstroth, Hopkins, Bridgman, 1853.

One Henderson seed catalogue, 1874.

One small silver statue of a running horse, inscription engraved under the base: *Otto Hasendorfer, silversmith, New Orleans, 1860.*

One red cotton headscarf.

One gold and red silk turban cloth.

One torn lace handkerchief.

A cast-iron kettle and a flat stone that served as a hot plate.

One black satin mourning dress with matching bonnet.

One tin of dried sassafras chips.

Sheet music, lyrics in French:

A la claire fontaine, m'en allant promener
J'ai trouvé l'eau si belle
Que je m'y suis baignée
Il y a longtemps que je t'aime, jamais je ne t'oublierai.

Sheet music:

Sonata in A-Major KV 526 for piano and violin
Wolfgang Amadeus Mozart
Allegro molto
Andante
Presto

A copy of the magazine *Beadle's Dime Novels*, featuring the science-fiction tale "Steam Man of the Prairies," by Edward S. Ellis.

One issue of *Harper's Weekly*, dated June 4, 1864.

One Pierrot puppet on strings, hardwood, face paint faded, white silk costume, jacket with three large black buttons, white ruff.

One ten-foot pole from a lumber flatboat.

One wooden box of handmade fishing lures, leather, fur, and feathers.

One metal box with key containing the framed photograph of a young woman in a wedding dress, a dried rose, an eighteenth-century pistol, and a deed to some land in North Carolina. The key, which is inserted into the lock, is attached to a thin leather cord.

Sketchbook signed *Simone (Rainy) Barnes* containing various watercolors of wild flowers, a cornfield, a vegetable garden with pumpkins and tomatoes. One pencil sketch of a woman playing the piano with the inscription *Maman*; one of a man reading on the front porch of a farmhouse with the inscription *Papa Will.*